# Hugo Pepper

# Hugo
# Pepper

# Paul Stewart & Chris Riddell

DOUBLEDAY

LONDON • NEW YORK • TORONTO • SYDNEY • AUCKLAND

HUGO PEPPER

A DOUBLEDAY BOOK 978 0 385 60725 4 (from January 2007)

0 385 60725 3

Published in Great Britain by Doubleday,
an imprint of Random House Children's Books

This edition published 2006

1 3 5 7 9 10 8 6 4 2

Set in Baltic Times by Palimpsest Book Production Limited, Polmont, Stirlingshire

RANDOM HOUSE CHILDREN'S BOOKS
61-63 Uxbridge Road, London W5 5SA
a division of The Random House Group Ltd

RANDOM HOUSE AUSTRALIA (PTY) LTD
20 Alfred Street, Milsons Point, Sydney,
New South Wales 2061, Australia

RANDOM HOUSE NEW ZEALAND LTD
18 Poland Road, Glenfield, Auckland 10, New Zealand

RANDOM HOUSE (PTY) LTD
Isle of Houghton, Corner of Boundary Road & Carse O'Gowrie,
Houghton 2198, South Africa

THE RANDOM HOUSE GROUP Limited Reg. No. 954009
www.kidsatrandomhouse.co.uk

A CIP catalogue record for this book is available from the British Library.

Printed and bound in Italy

*To Jack, Katy and Anna*

TREACLE

THE HARBOUR

CYCLOPS POINT
LIGHTHOUSE.

SLEEPING
HORSE
LANE

EVESHAM'S WORKSHOP

THE INSTITUTE

THE SOU

FIREFL

THE INSTIT

# Part One

"They lived in a little cabin deep in the
ice forests of the Frozen North . . ."

# The Snow Giant's Gift

Once upon a time, there were two reindeer herders called Harvi and Sarvi Runter-Tun-Tun. Harvi was tall and bony, Sarvi was short and round. Both of them had beady eyes, snub noses and long hair, which they tied up and kept hidden beneath their three-pointed reindeer herder hats.

HARVI RUNTER-TUN-TUN

They loved each other dearly and, though they were not blessed with children, they were happy and healthy, and counted themselves the luckiest reindeer herders in the whole wide world.

SARVI RUNTER-TUN-TUN

3

They lived in a little cabin deep in the ice forests of the Frozen North, where the summers are short and the winters are very, very long. Every summer, Harvi and Sarvi milked their reindeer beneath the midnight sun. Then, as the days grew short and the nights grew long, they would return to their cabin in the ice forests.

There, all through the long winter, beneath the ice moon, they made reindeer cheese – the finest in the whole of the Frozen North.

MOOSE-MILK MOZZARELLA

ELK GORGONZOLA

People came from far and wide just to taste their 'moose-milk mozzarella' and 'elk gorgonzola', while their famous 'red nose brie' was once served to no less a person than Queen Rita at a fabulous banquet aboard the *S.S. Euphonia*.

If they had wanted to, Harvi and Sarvi could have sold every truckle of reindeer cheese they produced,

REDNOSE BRIE HARVI & SARVI

but they didn't. And this is the reason why. Although they were famous cheesemakers, the Runter-Tun-Tuns were simple reindeer herders at heart and were always careful to observe the ways of the Frozen North.

One of those ways was to save a single truckle from every batch of cheese and leave it outside the cabin door last thing before going to bed. This was to keep the snow giants who lived in the ice forests happy. Neither Harvi nor Sarvi had ever actually seen a snow giant, but they both knew that they existed because they'd seen their giant footprints in the snow. These footprints were huge – as wide as a milk pail and with three long toes splayed out at the front of each massive foot.

So, as every reindeer herder knew, it made sense to keep such fearsome creatures happy. Each night, the Runter-Tun-Tuns left the cheese outside and each morning there would be cheese crumbs on the cabin doorstep and huge footprints which led off into the forest of ice. Sometimes the snow giants would leave little presents of their own, like sprigs of icicle-trees or a frozen fir-cone or two. As the wolves howled at the moon and hungry polar bears prowled in the distance, Harvi and Sarvi felt protected by their snow giants.

Along with the sprigs and fir-cones, the Runter-Tun-Tuns believed that the snow giants also brought them luck. Then, one dark snowy night, the snow giants brought Harvi and Sarvi something else. When Sarvi opened the door to their cabin and looked down – expecting to see cheese crumbs and a frozen fir-cone or two – she found herself looking into two bright twinkling blue eyes. She gave a high-pitched squeak of surprise, because there on the doorstep in the early light of dawn was a little baby wrapped up tightly in a blanket.

She knelt down, scooped the baby up in her arms and hugged it tightly. It gurgled contentedly.

Then she turned and rushed back inside, calling excitedly to her husband, 'Harvi! Harvi! Wake up! Look what the snow giants have brought us!'

Now the Runter-Tun-Tuns might have been simple reindeer herders at heart, but they knew that where there was a baby, there had to be parents somewhere close by. So Harvi put on his snow shoes, packed up a reindeer and set off to search the ice forests.

It was late afternoon with the low sun casting long shadows when he stumbled across it.

A strange sled, overturned, half-draped in a sheet of silk - and covered in polar bear claw marks. Next to it was all that was left of the baby's parents.

A gentleman's boot and a lady's glove.

There were polar bear tracks and snow-giant footprints in the snow, and the telltale signs of a mighty struggle. Harvi rolled up the silk sheet and turned the sled back over. Then - along with the gentleman's boot and the lady's glove - he stashed the sheet behind the seat, hitched the sled to his reindeer and towed it back to the cabin. There he stored it carefully at the back of the milking shed and went inside to tell Sarvi the sad news.

And it *was* sad news. But deep down, both Harvi and Sarvi were also happy, because now they had a little boy to call their own. His real parents may have been eaten by polar bears, but the snow giants had saved the baby and brought him to the Runter-Tun-Tuns, and they felt proud and honoured to have been chosen for the special task of raising the infant.

They also felt a little bit guilty, because although they loved the little baby and looked after him as if he was their own, teaching him about reindeer herding and cheesemaking and the ways of the Frozen North – and even called him by the name stitched into the back of the cardigan they found him in, there was one thing they *didn't* do.

They didn't try to find out where he came from.

Harvi and Sarvi knew they should have, but they were just simple reindeer herders and they were frightened of losing their little boy. So when people arrived from far-flung places to buy their cheese, the Runter-Tun-Tuns didn't ask or answer any questions. They simply smiled and nodded and wrapped up the truckles to keep them fresh – and always, always made sure that there was one left over for the snow giants.

And the years passed . . .

Then one day, ten and a half years later, the boy didn't come in from milking. When Harvi went to the milking shed, he found him at the very back, behind the woodpile, staring at the battered sled that had lain hidden there for all those years. He was holding a lady's glove in one hand and a gentleman's boot in the other.

# Chapter One

A heavy fog lay over the streets and alleyways of Harbour Heights, muffling the sounds and obscuring the sights of the town. In the distance, the mournful boom of the foghorn at Mermaid Cove could just be heard, while down by the harbour, the old disused lighthouse at

Cyclops Point had all but disappeared in a grey haze.

In the lower town, the shops along Archduke Ferdinand Boulevard were closing early and a trickle of theatre-goers was coming out of the matinée performance of *Fedrun Follies* at the Archduke Ferdinand Theatre.

In the upper town, there was an eerie quiet in the large elegant squares and spacious gardens of the Heights, most people preferring to stay indoors rather than walk the gloomy streets.

Anyone venturing out that foggy evening would have found Montmorency Square deserted, and not a soul to be seen on Clifftop Row. Turning right and climbing the three hundred steps of Sleeping Horse Lane, they would also have found themselves completely alone. But by turning left at the top of the steps into a forgotten little square far from the usual hustle and bustle of Harbour Heights, they would have encountered a curious figure looming out of the fog.

Tall and thin, and dressed in a shabby grey coat and a stovepipe hat, the old man *tap-tap-tapped* his way slowly around the little square, a long pole clasped in his gnarled hand.

Pausing beneath a tall, fluted lamppost, the old man raised the pole, gently unlatched the door of the lamp and pulled it open. Then he pressed gently down on the nozzle inside with the tip of the pole. There was a *click* followed by a soft *hiss* as the gas began to flow. Taking a taper from the brim of the tall hat, the lamplighter lit it with a flick of his thumb and placed it in the holder on the end of the pole.

Slowly and carefully he raised the glowing pole and held it over the nozzle inside the lamp. There was a muffled *pop*, followed by a flash of blue, which became a soft, yellow light as the mantle began to glow. The lamplighter pushed the glass door shut, the golden light gleaming on the beads of mist that encrusted his thick, droopy moustache, and moved on – *tap-tap-tap* – to the next lamppost.

Behind him a trail of soft, yellow lights twinkled out of the fog and, as if in answer, something remarkable happened. The untidy tangle of trees, shrubs and bushes of the garden in the middle of the square began to shimmer and twinkle. By the time the old lamplighter had lit the last lamp and *tap-tapped* his way back down Sleeping Horse Lane, the gardens were alive with thousands of dancing, shimmering fireflies. It was a magical sight, even on that gloomy evening – or at least, it would have been if there had been anyone around to see it.

Just then, out of the fog, there came a strange, stuttering sound, soft at first, but growing louder with every passing second.

*Phut! Phut! Splutter-splutter! Phut!*

It seemed to be coming from high up above the square – the sound of a little engine, spluttering and backfiring.

*Phut! Phut! Bang! Phut!* . . .

Just as it seemed to be directly over the gardens with their shimmering, twinkling fireflies, the engine cut out and, for a moment, there was complete silence. Then suddenly there came a whistling *whoosh* as something heavy fell from the sky. It crashed into a tall tree in the corner of the gardens with a loud *clang* and the sound of splintering branches.

With screeches of dismay, a dozen scruffy yellow cats shot out of the surrounding bushes and dashed off into the fog in the direction of

Sleeping Horse Lane, as a large silk balloon tumbled gracefully from the sky and crumpled over a splintered branch with a sigh. All was quiet for a moment. Then, accompanied by a soft rustling noise, the tree began to shake. Suddenly, a small bundle dropped from its branches and fell in a shower of leaves and fireflies.

As it reached the ground, the bundle hovered momentarily, then seemed to unfurl like a flower opening its petals, before settling gently on the damp earth. In the middle of the blanket, curled into a tight ball, was the figure of a small boy.

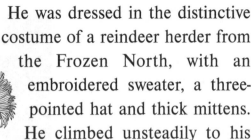

He was dressed in the distinctive costume of a reindeer herder from the Frozen North, with an embroidered sweater, a three-pointed hat and thick mittens. He climbed unsteadily to his feet and peered up at the tree, then down at the worn blanket on which he was standing. Kneeling down, he gently rolled the blanket up, put it under one arm and stumbled out of the garden on wobbly legs – straight into the path of two old ladies who had just come out of Sleeping Horse Lane.

They were tall, thin and elegantly dressed in long, flowing skirts that reached to the ground. Both had luxuriant bronze-coloured hair done up in elaborate

coils and buns, and each wore large, green-tinted spectacles through which they peered at the boy.

'Good evening, young man,' said the first old lady.

'Are you quite all right?' said the second old lady, looking at the boy's face, which was deathly white.

'I . . . I . . . haven't eaten for days . . .' the boy began, swaying on his feet. 'The cheese ran out . . . I had no idea it was this far from the Frozen North . . .'

'Cheese?' said the first old lady, putting down the lump of driftwood she was carrying.

'Frozen North?' said the second old lady, setting down the large seashell she had under her arm.

In front of them, the gardens shimmered in the thinning fog.

'Where . . . is this?' asked the boy unsteadily.

'Why,' the old ladies beamed at him through their green-tinted spectacles, 'Firefly Square, of course.'

But the boy didn't hear them, for he had fainted clean away.

"Once, they even found a bicycle and took it in turns
to ride it along the beach at Mermaid Cove."

# The Story Collector and the Mermaids

*O*nce upon a time, there were two young mermaids called Daisy and Lily Neptune. They swam in the seas around the pretty little fishing town of Harbour Heights, and lived in a damp cave hidden behind a curtain of seaweed fronds amongst the rocks of Mermaid Cove.

Now, it is often believed that mermaids spend all their time at the bottom of the ocean living in palaces of coral, and waited on hand and tail by brightly coloured fish. Some do, of course, but they are mostly mermaid royalty and appear in fairytales in which they make a big fuss about going on dry land.

DAISY NEPTUNE

LILY NEPTUNE

Daisy and Lily weren't like that at all. No, they were pretty ordinary mermaids really. They enjoyed swimming in the sea of course, but thought nothing of taking a walk along the sand when they felt like it. In fact, they actually enjoyed going for walks, much in the same way that people who live on land enjoy going for a swim.

They were extremely competent walkers, with highly developed tail fins and an efficient stepping-action. Both of them wore long, elegant walksuits especially made for walking. Truth be told, Daisy and Lily liked nothing better than strolling along the beach and collecting things that had been washed up there.

They used the flotsam and jetsam that they collected to decorate their cave, making it as cosy and inviting as a damp cave hidden behind a curtain of seaweed fronds ever could be. They found all sorts of interesting things, like rusty ships' bells, sea chests covered in barnacles and ornately carved figureheads. Once, they even found a bicycle and took it in turns to ride it along the beach at Mermaid Cove. It was there that they were spotted

by a pot-holer and musical dramatist called Edward T. Trellis, who never forgot the sight.

But that's another story . . .

Anyway, the reason Daisy and Lily found so much flotsam and jetsam on the beaches near Harbour Heights was because the coastline there was extremely rocky and ships were always getting wrecked, or running aground, or losing bits of themselves. The lighthouse at Cyclops Point had been built to help guide ships into the harbour, and had worked well when Harbour Heights had been a little fishing town. But the town had grown and, as more and more ships visited it, the seas around the coast got busier and busier.

The Cyclops Point lighthouse grew too small for such a big town whose harbourside lights could now be seen for miles. Along the coast at Mermaid Cove, however, it was a different matter, and hardly a month went by without a shipwreck of some kind of other. The townspeople knew that something had to be done, but couldn't decide what.

Some said Cyclops Point lighthouse should be pulled down and a new, taller lighthouse built. Others said it should be moved. And some said the whole town should move instead. No one could agree.

It looked like stalemate in Harbour Heights – with the number of wrecked ships increasing all the time – until a young local man by the name of Wilfred McPherson decided to take the matter in hand. A writer by profession, he also loved collecting stories. He decided to talk to every sea captain and fisherman who visited the harbour.

WILFRED McPHERSON

He listened to their stories of where the worst rocks and strongest currents were, and he collected them all together. Then, by studying the stories and comparing one with another, he came to an interesting conclusion, which he set out to test by setting sail in his small boat.

The story collector hadn't got far when a violent storm blew up and he found his boat being tossed about on huge waves. He was almost as good a sailor as he was a collector of stories, but even *he* couldn't stop his boat being dashed against the treacherous rocks of Mermaid Cove.

That would have been the end of the story, if it hadn't been for Daisy and Lily Neptune. They dived into the stormy sea and saved the story collector from drowning – just like those mermaids in fairytales – and brought him back to their damp cave. There, they showed him all the flotsam and jetsam they'd collected, including the bicycle, which only convinced the story collector all the more that his theory was right – that there needed to be a lighthouse at Mermaid Cove, on the rocks outside Daisy and Lily's home.

The story collector hurried back to Harbour

Heights (on Daisy's bicycle which, by the way, he didn't steal, but Daisy lent him, contrary to the scene in Edward T. Trellis's musical farce, *The Cycling Fish*.) There, he showed the Harbour Board his collection of sailors' stories, and told them all about his own shipwreck on the rocks of Mermaid Cove. He didn't, though, tell them about Daisy and Lily, because mermaids are extremely shy and retiring, and he knew they wouldn't want a fuss to be made of them.

The Harbour Board was convinced, and immediately set about building the new lighthouse at Mermaid Cove. It proved a great success. The Harbour Board and the townspeople – not to mention the sea captains and fishermen – were so grateful, that they rewarded him with a large sum of money and a small plot of land called Firefly Field, which was situated at the top of Sleeping Horse Lane.

There he built a little square, founded the Institute of Travellers' Tales, which later became home to *The Firefly Quarterly* – and married a beautiful young woman called Molly. They had met in front of the old lighthouse at Cyclops Point – which by then had been closed down – and fallen in love at first sight.

They lived happily in the prosperous and increasingly bustling city of Harbour Heights where, in due course, they had a beautiful baby daughter of their own, whom they named Phyllida. And at her christening, there were two strikingly elegant ladies in long walksuits and green spectacles who were delighted to become the baby's 'mermaid' godmothers.

# Chapter Two

## FEDRUN FOLLIES STAR A HIRSUTE FRAUD!

It has come to the attention of this magazine that all is not well at the Archduke Ferdinand Theatre. Quantities of hair tonic and expensive beard-restorer have been delivered in an atmosphere of utmost secrecy, not to mention the engagement of the services of a top-class scalp masseur.

And what can this hairy expense be for, you ask? Can it be that the celebrated Cuthbert Lionsmane is not all he might seem? Rumours reaching the Quarterly suggest the "Fedrun Follies" star is hiding an extremely bald secret!

*The Firefly Quarterly, Page 32*

lliot de Mille, editor of *The Firefly Quarterly*, stood looking out of the large oval window of his office. The glass panes had been white-washed, leaving two small eye-holes in the centre of the window for the director to spy, unobserved, on the comings and goings in Firefly Square.

ELLIOT de MILLE

It had been a usual sort of evening. That stuck-up girl from the carpet shop had walked her yappy little dog. Those busybodies from the teashop had closed early. And the ridiculous Neptune sisters had stopped to talk to some scruffy urchin. Now, that madman from the workshop had gone into the gardens.

'What's that darned fool doing climbing trees at his age?' he muttered to himself, tapping his two front teeth with the tip of his propelling pencil. 'He's going to break his neck if he's not careful . . .'

Outside, in the gardens at the middle of the square, a figure in a long, oil-stained apron and pointy slippers of unusual design, was halfway up a tall tree. Several broken branches and a scattering of leaves lay at the foot of the tree into whose leafy upper branches the figure now disappeared. The tree began to shake violently.

'Still,' said Elliot de Mille with a thin smile. 'If he did, it would save me the trouble.'

He turned away from the window, crossed the floor of the large office and sat himself down at an enormous roll-top desk. For a moment, he looked down at the dozen or so scraps of paper spread out neatly on the tooled green leather of the desk's surface and tapped his front teeth again with his pencil. Then, narrowing his eyes and leaning closer, Elliot de Mille examined a crumpled piece of paper before him.

'*Harbour Heights School Report*,' he muttered, an unpleasant smirk playing on his thin lips. '*Theodore Luscombe*,' he read on. 'Tut-tut-tut, Master Luscombe,' he said with a shake of his head. 'Must do better . . .'

Elliot leaned forward and took a sheet of crisp lined paper from one of the drawers of his enormous desk and licked the tip of his propelling pencil. Then, settling himself comfortably in his enormous leather swivel-chair, the director bent over and began to write.

It wasn't long before the paper was filled with a spidery scrawl. Elliot held it up and read and

 re-read it several times, his small eyes glinting malevolently from behind his wire-rimmed spectacles. When he was satisfied, he swivelled round and stamped heavily three times on the floor. Then he stood up, crossed to the window once more and peered out.

Firefly Square was deserted – but there was a trail of twigs and leaves leading through the gardens towards the small row of shops on the south side. The director tapped his teeth irritably with his propelling pencil as he read the signs on the shop fronts facing him across the little square.

'*Evesham's Workshop*; *Dalle and Daughter: Carpet Restorers*; *Camomile and Camomile: Tea Blenders* and *Neptune's Nautical Antiques*. Soon,' he whispered, 'all of you will be mine . . .'

Just then there was a faint knock on the door.

'Enter!' barked Elliot de Mille, the director, without turning round. Slowly the door creaked open. 'The stories for the next issue are on my desk,' he said.

"She soon became the wealthiest, most notorious
pirate captain of them all . . ."

# *The Beautiful Sea-Bed*

Once upon a time, there was a bold and beautiful pirate called Brimstone Kate. She sailed the seas from the Iceberg Straits of the Frozen North to the steamy waters of the Dandoon Delta, striking fear into all she came across. She soon became the wealthiest, most notorious pirate captain of them all, with a fortune in treasure which she kept under her bed in her cabin. After a while this became a problem, because her bed just wasn't big enough, and sleeping on top of piles of pearls and gold pieces and awkwardly shaped treasure of all kinds was extremely uncomfortable.

So, Brimstone Kate put in to the sleepy little fishing town of Harbour Heights and went in search of a blacksmith. She found one hard at work, making a lamp for the lighthouse that was at that time being built at Cyclops Point, and persuaded him to stop what he was doing to make her a new bed. Now, because he was a clever blacksmith, and

because he was being paid by the hour, he made sure that he took a very long time over Brimstone Kate's bed. This meant that by the time he had finished, the bed was the most ornate, beautifully made bed that anyone had ever seen.

Brimstone Kate was delighted with it, even if it had been extremely expensive *and* caused her crew no end of trouble as they'd struggled to get it into her cabin. She was able to store her treasure neatly underneath it - and even had space for

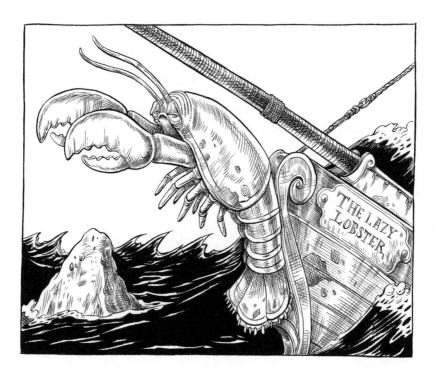

several pairs of shoes and a cutlass or two. Unfortunately, the blacksmith had taken so long making the beautiful sea-bed that he hadn't got round to finishing the lamp for the Cyclops Point lighthouse and, not long after, Brimstone Kate's ship ran into the rocks outside Harbour Heights and sank.

Nothing was heard of Brimstone Kate from that day forth – although there were rumours that she had somehow managed to escape with her treasure and had returned to Harbour Heights, where she married the handsome lighthouse keeper of the brand new Cyclops Point lighthouse and had a daughter named Molly.

# Chapter Three

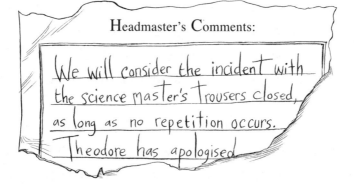

We will consider the incident with the science master's trousers closed, as long as no repetition occurs. Theodore has apologised

ugo Pepper opened one eye; then the other. He looked around. He was lying in the middle of an enormous wrought-iron bed, his head sunk deep into a soft downy pillow. Above him, iron branches which reached almost to the ceiling curled and criss-crossed, each one covered in intricate furling leaves and delicately wrought fruits.

At the foot of the bed, through the curving ironwork, he could glimpse daylight streaming in through the shutters of a little window.

The bed felt warm and soft after the hard, padded bench of the strange sled. Hugo rolled over, sank his face into the downy pillow and breathed in its soft scent of sea-jasmine and briny-lavender.

As he did so, he pictured Harvi and Sarvi's faces when they had told him the story of how they'd found him – a story he would never have been told at all if he hadn't stumbled across the strange battered sled in the milking shed; the sled that had belonged to his real parents.

To Hugo, though, Harvi and Sarvi would always be his parents, because it was they who had raised him, teaching him about reindeer herding and cheesemaking and the ways of the Frozen North. They loved him – their 'Gift from the Snow Giants', as they called him – and he loved them. He could happily have stayed with them for ever in the forests of the Frozen North, and would have, had it not been for the mysterious 'Compass of the Heart'.

Hugo's own heart had started thumping the moment he had seen it in the gloom of the milking shed. It was round and shiny and situated just next to a lever with *Start-Stop* embossed at its base.

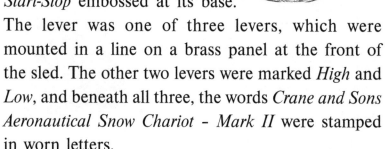

The lever was one of three levers, which were mounted in a line on a brass panel at the front of the sled. The other two levers were marked *High* and *Low*, and beneath all three, the words *Crane and Sons Aeronautical Snow Chariot - Mark II* were stamped in worn letters.

Intriguing as this all was, it wasn't enough to start Hugo's heart thumping like a snow rabbit on thin ice. No, it was the sight of the round, shiny 'Compass of the Heart' that did that. From the moment Hugo saw the destination needle and read the words on the dial, he knew exactly what he had to do.

Of course, Harvi and Sarvi were shocked when he told them, but they loved him and still felt guilty that they had neither told Hugo about his real parents nor tried to find out more about them.

So, in the end, they agreed to help him get the aeronautical snow chariot working again. Sarvi repaired the silk balloon. Harvi cleaned the little steam engine as best he could and greased its propeller. Hugo gathered logs in the ice forest for the little boiler, and thawed them out. It wasn't long before everything was ready.

Hugo turned over in the enormous bed and stared up at the ceiling. Leaving Harvi and Sarvi and his home in the Frozen North had been hard, and tears came to his eyes just thinking about it.

But he'd *had* to.

He curled up into a tight ball as he remembered climbing into the snow chariot, pulling his blanket round his shoulders – the very one his real parents had wrapped him in – and pushing the first lever to *Start*.

The chariot's steam engine had rumbled and wheezed, and the patchwork balloon had filled with hot air. Slowly, unsteadily, the chariot had risen up from the ground as Harvi and Sarvi waved, scalding tears streaming down their cheeks.

Hugo had peered down at the 'Compass of the Heart'. The destination needle was fixed on *The Frozen North*. With trembling fingers he turned the small dial round, past *The Exotic East*, past *The Sunny South*, towards *The Wild West* and on to the word on the dial that had made his heart thump so when he'd first read it.

The snow chariot gave a lurch forward and rose higher in the sky. It gained speed steadily and was soon leaving the ice forests of the Frozen North far behind, its compass set on *Home*.

High over the jagged peaks of ice mountains Hugo flew in the strange aeronautical snow chariot, its engine wheezing and spluttering and the patched silk balloon billowing overhead. Soon, the snow sheets gave way to the vast expanse of icy oceans that seemed to stretch on for ever.

On the third day - by which time Hugo had finished the last of his cheese and was stiff and cold and wishing he was back in his warm, comfortable cabin with Harvi and Sarvi - he almost gave up. He stared at the 'Compass of the Heart'. One turn of the dial to *The Frozen North*, and he could return.

But then he would never find out anything about his real parents; who they were, what they did, or anything about the place that *they* called home.

Hugo had gritted his teeth, clenched his fists and pulled his blanket tightly around him. He wasn't going to give up . . .

Just then, there was a knock on the door and a head poked round into the bedroom. It belonged to an old lady with green spectacles and a mass of bronze-coloured hair done up in buns and coils.

'I see you're awake, young man.' She smiled at Hugo. 'Slept well, I hope. You should have. After all, this is the beautiful sea-bed that once belonged to Brimstone Kate, the pirate. Daisy and I found it at the bottom of the harbour – had a terrible job getting it back to the shop, I can tell you . . .'

'Oh, Lily, the young man doesn't want to know all that.' A second head appeared round the door. 'Here, I've brought you a cup of Camomiles' special *Pick-Me-Up* tea. It'll do you the world of good. I'm Daisy Neptune, and this is my sister, Lily. She's the talkative one,' she added with a little laugh. 'Always has been, ever since we were tiddlers . . .'

'I'm Hugo,' said Hugo, sitting up in bed. 'Hugo Pepper.'

There were two gasps, followed by the sound of a full teacup smashing on the floor.

"He had long since moved on from plain inventing,
and was now dabbling in mechanical wizardry."

# The Mechanical Wizard

*O*nce upon a time, there was a young engineer called Edward Evesham. Ever since he could remember, he had loved all things mechanical. Bird-feeders, candle-snuffers, envelope-openers, toasting-machines – you name it, young Edward had made them in his workshop as a boy, and when he was old enough, he joined the firm of *Crane and Sons* as a junior designer in the Lighting and Related Appliances Department.

There, he soon made a name for himself with his work on the *Crane and Sons* reading lamp

and the more exotic retractable bath light with illuminated soap-dish. You see, what Edward liked most in the world was to take an invention and improve on it in unexpected and surprising ways.

Of course, the reading lamp didn't *need* to shine more brightly the more exciting the reader found the book he was reading, and the retractable bath light didn't *need* an illuminated soapdish that sank when the bath water became cold. But Edward enjoyed his work and liked nothing more than rising to the challenge of his own inventive imagination.

At first, his career with *Crane and Sons* went well – so well, in fact, that Edward was promoted to the Special Projects Department. Here he worked on some really interesting things you probably won't have heard of.

There was the *Crane and Sons Self-Propelling Deckchair* which was a special commission for the *S.S. Euphonia*. And a top-secret flying horse built for none other than old man Crane himself. Unfortunately, this is where the trouble started for Edward.

You see, he just couldn't resist adding his own little touches to whatever invention he was working on at the time. Giving the flying horse a head for heights was ingenious, but giving the deckchair the ability to leap twenty feet in the air nearly caused a nasty incident on the *S.S. Euphonia*'s maiden voyage involving Queen Rita's pet spaniel, Mitzi.

Edward was called into old man Crane's office and made to promise, in front of him and his son, Theodore, not to make any more 'improvements' without permission. Theodore was sympathetic to Edward because he was an inventor himself and recognized this talent in others, but even *he* felt

51

that the line had to be drawn somewhere.

Although Edward did promise, he really couldn't help himself. He had long since moved on from plain inventing, and was now dabbling in mechanical wizardry.

Now, mechanical wizardry, for those of you who don't already know, is where engineering and magic mix. Many inventors don't believe in it, and others are not so persuaded by its practical use – but not Edward. And, as an enthusiastic advocate of mechanical wizardry, he was soon experimenting with mystical bolts and self-tightening screws, emotional bookshelves and invisible lampstands. A lot of this was hare-brained and crackpot, but every now and then, Edward would make a breakthrough. His self-correcting fountain pen proved a boon to bad spellers everywhere, while his ear-piece especially designed for the hard of understanding was a marvel . . .

But for every success, there was a setback, and it was one of these – the self-improving kettle – which proved to be his downfall. The kettle judged and improved upon its performance every time it boiled, but it turned out to be too self-critical and a number of them blew themselves up in fits of despair.

Edward was asked to leave the firm of *Crane and Sons*, his promising career in tatters. Theodore Crane was very sorry to let him go, but old man Crane's mind was made up. The wayward young inventor would have to leave.

In a final act of kindness, however, Theodore Crane recommended Edward to a young explorer called Phineas Pepper who was looking for an engineer to work on a special contraption he'd just taken delivery of. The young explorer was delighted, and set Edward to work at once, modifying and improving the *Crane and Sons Aeronautical Snow Chariot - Mark II*, in preparation for Phineas Pepper's maiden flight.

# Chapter Four

## HEIR TO UMBRELLA FORTUNE GETS A SOAKING!

The Quarterly has heard rumours that the Luscombe family, of H.H. Luscombe, makers of fine umbrellas, is none too pleased with its youngest member.

Theodore Luscombe Jnr. set his science master's trousers on fire as they hung on the washing line, only to receive a soaking as the said trousers were extinguished by an extremely cross headmaster. Look out for further revelations of young Luscombe's career shortly!

*The Firefly Quarterly, Page 20*

ugo had seen nothing like the interior of *Neptune's Nautical Antiques* before. Harvi and Sarvi's small cabin in the ice forests of the Frozen North was cluttered, and Hugo was always tripping over milk buckets or hitting his head on hanging ladles, but that was nothing compared to the sight which greeted him as he followed Daisy and Lily Neptune down the stairs.

There were curious and fascinating objects everywhere he looked: jawbones of immense fish, seashells of every size and description, brass ships' fittings and driftwood, carved into extraordinary designs and fashioned into ingenious furniture.

On one wall, like the trophies of a big-game hunter, were the sculpted figureheads of a dozen ships; on another, a bewildering array of anchors and grappling hooks. Glass fishermen's floats, some suspended in draped web-like nets, hung from the ceiling alongside portholes, nautical lanterns and several huge harpoons. The driftwood tables and sideboards groaned beneath the weight of deck-quoits and cannon balls, chunks of coral and strings of razor-sharp sharks' teeth. Littering the floor were coils of

anchor chains and stacks of barnacle-encrusted sea chests, which created an intricate maze through which Daisy and Lily picked their way, their long dresses swishing as they trailed along the floor.

'Welcome to *Neptune's Nautical Antiques*,' said Daisy brightly, settling herself at one of the least cluttered tables and picking up a large teapot with an anchor printed on its lid.

'I can't tell you how delighted we are to have found you,' said Lily, joining her sister at the table and pulling up a sea chest for Hugo to sit on. She held out a teacup with an anchor design on it, while Daisy poured some tea, and offered it to him.

'You know, I find it endlessly fascinating,' she said thoughtfully. 'Some things which get lost at sea travel such immense distances, some remain on the sea bed precisely where they went down, while others . . .' She looked at Hugo through her large green spectacles. 'They wash up right back where they came from.' She smiled kindly. 'Come on now, Hugo, dear. Drink your tea before it gets cold.'

Hugo took a sip of the hot, sweet-tasting tea, and felt its warmth flow down into his stomach and along his arms and legs, right to the very tips of his fingers and toes. He took another sip. His scalp tingled and his cheeks flushed. It was the most delicious drink he'd ever tasted. All his strength seemed to be returning to him. Before he knew it, he'd drained the teacup to the dregs and Daisy was pouring him another.

'Camomiles' *Pick-Me-Up* tea,' she smiled. 'It never fails, Hugo, my dear.'

Hugo smiled back, then said, 'You seemed to recognize me when I told you my name.' He shifted about on the sea chest, which was covered in barnacles and rather uncomfortable. 'Are we related?'

The sisters exchanged looks with each other through their green spectacles.

'I suppose we are, in a way,' said Lily, lifting the hem of her long skirt and swishing her wide, fishy tail.

Hugo gasped. 'But you're a mermaid!' he exclaimed.

'Precisely,' Lily smiled. 'We were your mother's mermaid godmothers.'

'That's like fairy godmothers, but fishier,' added Daisy.

'My *mother*!' said Hugo, swallowing hard. 'Tell me about her. I never knew her, you see. She was eaten by polar bears and I was rescued by snow giants and brought up by reindeer herders . . .'

'Polar bears?' said Lily, tears glistening behind her green spectacles.

'Snow giants? Reindeer herders?' said Daisy, taking off her own spectacles and dabbing at her eyes. 'We feared the worst. We begged her not to go . . . But she wouldn't listen. Headstrong, she was, just like dear Wilfred, her father . . . And now, after all these years . . .'

Lily grabbed Hugo and hugged him tightly.

'Phyllida was headstrong, certainly,' she sobbed. 'But she was also beautiful and brave, and loved collecting stories . . .'

'Just like her father,' interrupted Daisy.

Lily hugged Hugo even tighter. 'And she must have loved you very, very much.'

Hugo looked up at Lily Neptune. He could see his own face reflected in her green spectacles.

'How do you know?' he said, in a small, croaky voice.

Lily's eyes filled with tears again. She let go of Hugo and picked up the blanket that had been lying, neatly rolled, beside the driftwood table.

'Because of this,' she said.

"There, he tended a flock of cloud sheep."

# The Cloud Sheep

*O*nce upon a time, there was a young shepherd called Lempik Dalle. He lived high up in the mountains of the Randoo Kush, where the grass is sweet and the air is thin. There, he tended a flock of cloud sheep.

Now, cloud sheep, for those of you who don't already know, are extremely small. In fact, they're no bigger than an average guinea pig, but in every other respect they look just like normal sheep. They have coats of thick, fluffy wool, and they graze on the blue grass that grows high up on the slopes of the Randoo Kush. They're called cloud sheep because, at a distance, and even quite close up, they look just like white clouds against the sky blue grass.

Lempik Dalle's cloud sheep were some of the best in the mountains and their wool was highly prized. Cloud sheep wool is so light that it actually floats. In fact, the most important part of the job of a shepherd like Lempik was to stop his flock being blown away on the mountain breeze. That's why cloud shepherds carried large nets (rather like butterfly collectors' nets) instead of crooks.

Cloud sheep wool was far too precious to be used in cardigans or scarves. Instead, it was used by the carpet weavers of the Randoo Kush in their extraordinary – some would say, magical – flying carpets.

Not only were Lempik Dalle's cloud sheep some of the best in the mountains, but he was also married to one of the finest carpet weavers in those parts. Now, for those of you who don't already know, flying carpets are extremely rare because it takes a lot of cloud sheep wool to make one, not to mention an extremely skilled weaver.

Most weavers use only a thread or two of actual cloud sheep wool in their so-called flying carpets, and very few ever made a carpet that was even half cloud sheep and half normal sheep wool. But Lempik Dalle's wife, Neena, regularly made carpets that were half-and-half, and once, she even made one of a hundred per cent pure cloud sheep wool – something that was practically unheard of.

Now, a half-and-half flying carpet won't actually fly as such, but it will float and it can certainly cushion a fall from a great height very effectively. The mountains of the Randoo Kush are extremely steep and people are always falling off them, which is why Neena Dalle's carpets were in high demand.

Then one day, an intrepid story collector called Wilfred McPherson arrived in the mountains.

He'd been heading for the Frozen North when his *Crane and Sons Aeronautical Snow Chariot - Mark I* had been blown off course by a terrible storm. Unfortunately, the terrible storm had also blown away every flock of cloud sheep in the Randoo Kush, including Lempik Dalle's. He and his wife were heartbroken – not to mention financially ruined.

When the story collector heard their tale, he suggested that they come home with him to the town of Harbour Heights and set up a carpet business there.

(Wilfred McPherson was always doing this sort of thing. Take the pygmy snowmen he came across in the Frozen North, for example. But that's another story.)

Anyway, that's just what Lempik and Neena Dalle did, and they lived very happily there. And when they retired to the Randoo Kush, their daughter, Meena, took over the shop – much to the joy of her best friend, Wilfred McPherson's daughter, Phyllida.

# Chapter Five

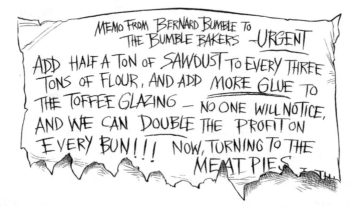

MEMO FROM BERNARD BUMBLE TO THE BUMBLE BAKERS —URGENT
ADD HALF A TON OF SAWDUST TO EVERY THREE TONS OF FLOUR, AND ADD MORE GLUE TO THE TOFFEE GLAZING — NO ONE WILL NOTICE, AND WE CAN DOUBLE THE PROFIT ON EVERY BUN!!! NOW, TURNING TO THE MEAT PIES...TH...

ugo followed Daisy and Lily Neptune as they swished out of *Neptune's Nautical Antiques*. Lily paused and turned the sign on the front door over to show 'Closed', before shutting it.

'Not that it matters,' said Daisy to Hugo gloomily. 'Business is *so* bad at the moment.'

Hugo was dressed in a large sou'wester, a stripy vest, wide canvas trousers and a nautical overcoat that was several sizes too big for him.

'It doesn't do to draw attention to oneself,' Daisy had told him, packing away his reindeer herder clothes. 'Not these days. It seems everybody gossips about everyone else, and not nice stories either . . .'

'The worse the better, in fact,' said Lily, casting an eye at the building opposite. 'And it's all the fault of *The Firefly Quarterly*.' She shuddered as she glided along the pavement to the shop next door but one. The sign above the doorway read *Dalle and Daughter: Rug Restorers*.

'It's probably better if you allow us to break the news to Meena,' whispered Daisy, pushing open the door and ushering Hugo inside. 'After all, she was your mother's best friend.'

Hugo took a deep breath and entered the shop.

It was dark and very quiet inside, with a heady perfumed scent in the air. Large ornately patterned carpets hung in rows from racks overhead, like a series of heavy curtains. In one corner, by the window, a tiny dog was reclining on a cushion. Its head was cocked to one side and it seemed to be looking intently at a space a few feet above where it lay. As Hugo watched, a small dusty coloured moth fluttered up from behind a carpet. Instantly, the little dog launched itself high in the air and caught the moth in its jaws with a single snap. Hugo blinked.

'That's Tik-Tik,' said Daisy, closing the shop door behind her. 'He's a moth-dog. No carpet shop should be without one.'

'Daisy? Is that you?' came a musical voice from a room at the back of the shop. 'Come on through – and bring that sister of yours with you.'

'We've brought someone special to see you, Meena, dear,' called Lily. 'But first, I've got some rather sad news to tell you.'

Lily swished past the carpets, brushing them aside, and disappeared into the back room. Daisy stood beside Hugo with a hand on his shoulder, while Tik-Tik snapped up several more moths that had been disturbed when they entered. A few moments later, Hugo heard a small scream, followed by some quieter sobbing, and Lily's voice saying, 'There, there, Meena, we did what we could . . .' Then, 'You'd better come through now, Hugo, dear.'

He felt Daisy's hand on his shoulder urging him on, so he pushed through the carpets and entered the back room. It was, he discovered, surprisingly large. The walls were lined with shelves on which were stacked rolls of carpets, balls of wool and racks of long darning needles. A large wooden frame took up most of the far wall, upon which a worn-looking carpet had been stretched.

And next to it – halfway between the floor and the ceiling – a woman hovered.

She had long hair, pulled back and plaited, and was wearing a smock and baggy trousers, which were gathered in at the ankle, and a pair of pointy carpet slippers of unusual design. Lily Neptune was sitting on a large wooden bench below her, polishing her green spectacles, with Hugo's blanket spread out at her tail.

As Hugo approached, the woman clicked her heels together and sank slowly to the floor to face him. Up close, Hugo could see she'd been crying. But she smiled bravely now as she ruffled his hair gently with one hand.

MEENA, DALLE &TIK·TIK

'So, you're Phyllida's little boy, are you?' she said. 'Yes, I can see the resemblance . . .' For a moment, Hugo thought she was going to burst into tears, but instead she continued, 'I'm Meena.

Your mother was my best friend. I begged her not to go on that last voyage with your father. We all knew it was headed for disaster, but she wouldn't listen – and, of course, she could never have left you behind.' Meena shook her head sadly. 'So I gave her one of my mother's finest flying carpets to keep her safe.'

'You mean the blanket I was wrapped up in is a flying carpet?' gasped Hugo, looking at the worn, threadbare fabric at Lily's tail.

'The finest cloud sheep wool, and at least half-and-half,' said Meena. 'Don't you see, Hugo? Your mother wrapped you up in it to keep you safe.'

Hugo nodded. There was a lump in his throat.

'But how did you know the voyage was headed for disaster?' he asked, bewildered. 'How could *anybody* possibly know my parents were going to be eaten by polar bears?'

'That, dear Hugo,' said Daisy, who'd been standing behind him, 'is a different cup of tea entirely.'

"She gave a small, ladylike gasp of surprise . . ."

# The Unexpected Teacup

*O*nce upon a time, there were two families who lived in a small valley in the Sunny South. They were called the Camomiles and the Mangerlaines, and they were always arguing. This was because they lived in a small valley and, although it was in the Sunny South, one side of the valley was usually sunnier than the other.

DON CAMOMILE

Now, ordinarily, this wouldn't have mattered, but the Camomiles and the Mangerlaines both grew tea. In fact, between them they grew fifty-eight different varieties of tea, all of which needed different amounts of sunlight to ripen. So the two families were always arguing over who had the right to plant their particular type of tea where and for how long.

SIGNORA MANGERLAINE

Families in the Sunny South can be extremely large, and the Camomiles and the Mangerlaines were no exception. Don Camomile had twenty sons, each of whom had ten children, who all grew up and had children of their own. Signora Mangerlaine had seven sons and eight daughters, who all did the same. So the small valley was getting pretty crowded, and the arguments, worse and worse. This wasn't helped by the fact that no Camomile ever married a Mangerlaine – or the other way round.

When it came for them to find partners, the young Camomiles and Mangerlaines set off for neighbouring valleys to court the sons and daughters of other families, who grew things like cucumbers or curly kale, or even, at a push – and only if they were desperate – coffee beans. Some of the daughters stayed in their new homes, but all of the sons returned with their young brides, and the valley got fuller and fuller.

Then one day, something unexpected happened. Freda, the youngest daughter of one of the Mangerlaine families, was invited to a tea dance in a valley close by which was devoted to marrow growing. By some terrible mix up, one of the

Camomile boys by the name of Diego, was invited too. During a short break between the tango and the foxtrot, Freda picked up her teacup and peered into it. She gave a small, ladylike gasp of surprise, for she had quite unexpectedly discovered she could read the tea-leaves at the bottom of the cup.

They told her that she was to marry the next man who asked her to dance. At that moment Diego Camomile tapped her politely on the shoulder and asked her to join him in the foxtrot, completely unaware that he was talking to a Mangerlaine. They started talking about tea varieties and blends as they danced, and by the time the waltz came round, and they discovered each other's surnames, it was already too late.

They were madly in love.

Of course, the two families were outraged when Diego and Freda announced their intention to marry, and they were forced to run away – aided by a kind explorer who had listened to their story. With his help, they travelled to the bustling town of Harbour Heights, where they set up a tea-blending business. Everything went well until one day, years later, just before Phineas and Phyllida Pepper were due to set off on a voyage for the Frozen North, Freda Camomile picked up her teacup and peered into it. This time, she let out a most unladylike shriek.

# Chapter Six

# DELICIOUS AT TWICE THE PRICE!

The Quarterly is delighted to announce a generous donation from Bernard Bumble's Buns and Pies, and can confirm that this fine old firm's products are as delicious as ever – if not more so!

Never fear though, Mr Bumble, the Quarterly will be watching and tasting to make sure your standards are maintained – along with those donations!

*The Firefly Quarterly, Page 17*

THE LAMPLIGHTER

*Tap-tap-tap!* The tall, thin figure of the lamplighter appeared at the top of Brimstone Alley and turned the corner into Firefly Square. He stopped by the lamppost outside *Camomile and Camomile: Tea Blenders* and carefully lit the lamp, before continuing on his way.

*Tap-tap-tap!*

'Good evening,' said Hugo Pepper politely, raising his sou'wester.

The lamplighter paused and regarded him with watery, grey eyes for a moment. Then, without so much as a word of greeting or a nod of acknowledgement, he moved on.

'Don't mind him, Hugo, dear,' said Daisy Neptune, as she swished past, and rang the bell outside the tea blenders. 'He never says a thing.'

'We haven't heard him speak in all the years we've lived in Firefly Square,' added Lily Neptune, swishing up behind. 'Not once.'

The door of the tea blenders was opened by a plump, jolly-faced man. He had wavy grey hair, a little moustache and, given the pudginess of his hands, curiously delicate fingers.

'Why, if it isn't my favourite ladies of the sea,' he beamed. 'Come in, come in! You're just in time for tea!'

'Thank you, Diego. We've brought a young visitor with us . . .'

'Phineas and Phyllida's boy! Yes, Freda told me to expect you, my dear boy,' said Diego Camomile, taking Hugo's hand and giving it a vigorous shake. 'I'm delighted to meet you. Come in, come in!'

DIEGO CAMOMILE

Hugo and the Neptune sisters followed Diego inside the shop while he called excitedly to his wife. Stepping over the threshold, Hugo found himself on the landing of a wrought-iron spiral staircase that rose to the shop's rafters and descended to its basement. The inside of *Camomile and Camomile* was one big space, into which were stacked tea chests which surrounded the spiral staircase from the bottom to the top.

Light came in from a large skylight in the roof, through which Hugo could see the fading splendour of a golden sunset. Next to it was a suspended wooden cabin, which Hugo supposed was the Camomiles' bedroom, while three non-existent floors down, there was the orange glow of a small stove, and a round table set with tea things. And at the table was a pale, delicate-looking woman with grey hair and a kind face. They all descended the stairs to join her, Diego calling down as they went.

'Freda, my love, he's here! Hugo Pepper's here! Just like you said!'

As Hugo Pepper climbed down the spiral staircase, he glanced at the labels stamped onto the stacked wooden tea chests he passed. *Rumbly Tummy. Bad Knee. Heartburn . . .*

'Medicinal blends on this side,' called Diego back over his shoulder.

Hugo nodded and turned the other way.

*Happy - Mild. Merry - Strong. Weepy - Moderate,* he read.

'Emotional teas on the other,' Diego informed him.

They reached the basement and joined Freda at the tea table. The tea chests surrounding them also had labels on them. *Near Future, Soon to Pass, Yet to Be,* they read, and *Not for Ages.*

'And these,' said Diego proudly, 'are the teas I blend especially for Freda.' He took a tiny teapot from the stove, shook it gently and poured its contents into his wife's teacup. 'Fortune-telling tea!'

He turned to the stove and picked up another, far larger teapot and poured everyone else a cup, before producing a plate of small cakes which filled the room with a delicious nutty, chocolatey, caramelly smell.

'For the rest of us, Camomiles' special *Heartfelt Welcome* blend,' he said. 'And what better to go with it than Archduke Ferdinand's Florentines, fresh from the *Fateful Voyage Bakery*!'

He beamed happily as Hugo took one and tasted it. The Florentine was delicious. He took a sip of tea. It seemed to slip down his throat and spread a wonderful warm feeling through his chest.

'Diego's teas are the finest in Harbour Heights,'

said Daisy. 'But people just don't seem to want to buy them any more.'

'It's that nasty *Firefly Quarterly* saying horrible untrue things about them,' said Lily fiercely.

'About *all* of us who don't make donations,' Daisy added bitterly.

'Please, ladies, let's not burden poor Hugo with our problems,' said Diego, trying to smile. 'After all, the poor boy's parents were eaten by polar bears . . . Poor Phineas and Phyllida.' He shook his head. 'And Freda tried so hard to warn them. She saw it all in the bottom of her teacup, didn't you, dear?'

But Mrs Camomile didn't answer her husband. She was too busy staring into her teacup, a trance-like expression on her face.

'What is it, Freda, dear?' asked Daisy and Lily both together. 'What do you see?'

Freda peered closely into the teacup and spoke,

her voice curiously high-pitched and warbly, like a surprised quail.

'I see a one-eyed giant,' she trilled, her eyes fixed on the tea-leaves at the bottom of the teacup, 'staring at a one-eared cat, pointing the way to the sea-bed's treasure.'

'What does that mean?' asked Hugo, deeply impressed.

Freda Camomile put down her cup and smiled brightly. 'I've absolutely no idea,' she said. 'Now, would somebody care to pass me a Florentine?'

"Unfortunately, Cressida wasn't a very good housemaid."

# The Cat Lady

*O*nce upon a time, there was a young housemaid called Cressida Claw. She worked at the fine houses in the big squares of the bustling city of Harbour Heights. Unfortunately, Cressida wasn't a very good housemaid. She was slovenly, bad-tempered and quite lazy, which meant that she never stayed in one job for more than a month or two at a time.

CRESSIDA CLAW

Before long, she had worked all over Harbour Heights and had got to know its squares and streets, alleyways and lanes extremely well – not to mention the houses, great and small, that lined them.

Cressida hated being a housemaid and resented having to sweep and clean and wash dishes and beat carpets. She hated all housework *and* the people she had to clear up after, with all their messy clutter and untidiness. In fact there was only one thing that

Cressida Claw actually liked about being a housemaid, and that was this . . .

She loved the opportunity it gave her for snooping.

Whenever the coast was clear, Cressida would lay down her mop or feather duster and start going through the belongings of the people she was supposed to be cleaning for. Cupboards, wardrobes, drawers and dressing-tables; nothing escaped Cressida Claw's nimble fingers or gimlet eyes. She would search through the pockets of overcoats hanging in the hall and sift through the waste-paper baskets.

Sometimes, she would even rummage in the dustbins in the back alleys. You see, what Cressida had discovered during her years as a housemaid in Harbour Heights, is that you never can tell what you might find if you have a good snoop.

Of course, the only trouble with snooping is that you could get caught. Cressida Claw was pretty good at snooping, but she got caught more often than she'd have liked, which – since people don't like snoopers – meant that she kept losing her job. But Cressida didn't mind too much, and she certainly learned some interesting things along the way, such as what to keep and what to leave when snooping.

Taking money or valuable jewellery usually led to trouble because they were bound to be missed. But anything that looked forgotten, or was likely to seem as if it had been lost, was fine. So Cressida took a lot of odd coins left in overcoat pockets, and single earrings from jewellery boxes. But the best things of all to take when snooping, she soon discovered, were things that seemed the least valuable to the untrained eye such as letters, scribbled notes, address books, laundry lists, reports and accounts of all kinds – anything, in fact, that might contain information.

Cressida soon found out that information was extremely valuable. People would pay for information. So that's what Cressida Claw sold.

She sold holiday dates to burglars, shopping lists to tradesmen, address books to insurance salesmen and confidence tricksters, and embarrassing love letters back to their owners. Unfortunately, Cressida soon acquired an extremely bad reputation as a housemaid – not only because she was very bad at housework, but because trouble seemed to follow her around. Finally, she found that she couldn't get a job anywhere.

Now, when Cressida had been unemployed in the past, she had spent a lot of her spare time snooping in the dustbins in the alleyways behind the large squares. And it was there that she'd made some unlikely friends. These were the scruffy yellow alley cats who lived there.

They took to following her about and going through the bins with her, for fish-heads and half-empty tin cans. Cressida grew to love them for their crafty ways and ability to sneak silently into those nooks and crannies that she could never reach. So when Cressida Claw found herself permanently out of work, she spent all her time with her beloved cats and slowly, bit by bit, she began to train them.

# Chapter Seven

---

≫ *Harbour Heights Nautical Savings Bank* ≪

27 Magdalene Walk, Harbour Heights

*re: Neptune's Nautical Antiques*

*Dear Miss Neptune and Miss Neptune,*

*Regrettably, it appears that your account with us is completely without funds, and we are therefore unable to lend you the sum you required.*

*Yours sincerely,*

*Lionel D. Pecksniff*

Deputy Manager

---

s the large silver moon rose above Firefly Square, all was quiet in the streets and gardens below. Apart from the lights which were still shining in *Evesham's Workshop*, all the other shops on the south side were in darkness, and had been for hours. The shuttered windows of the institute were similarly dark. This wasn't unusual. In fact, it was only when *The Firefly Quarterly* magazine was being printed that the windows of the institute blazed through the night – and that, for obvious reasons, was only four times a year.

A more regular occurrence – yet one which scarcely a soul had ever noticed – was taking place at that very moment on the roof of the institute, however. Lines of small, furry figures were emerging from the chimney pots and padding silently across the tiles, the moonlight glistening on their sooty heads. Soon, on three sides of Firefly Square, the rooftops of the institute were crowded with the little creatures. They jostled silently with each other, like seals on a crowded beach, as each found a place on the silvery roof tiles and lay down. Then, one after the other, in a curious ripple effect, they raised their large, furry feet in the air and gently wiggled their toes at the moon.

A short while later, Elliot de Mille, director of

the institute appeared at the top of the iron fire escape and stepped onto the roof. Ignoring the creatures that were lying on the slope of the roof behind him, the director strode to the edge of the low perimeter wall that ran the length of the institute's frontage, and waited.

Several minutes passed, and behind the director – who was dressed in patent-leather mules and a monogrammed silk dressing-gown – the creatures continued to wiggle their toes, humming contentedly as they did so. Suddenly losing patience, Elliot de Mille spun round.

'That's enough feet cooling!' he hissed. 'Back down the chimneys with you, now!'

The small creatures sat up and, in a spreading ripple, climbed to their feet. Then, slowly and reluctantly, they shuffled off towards the chimneys. One by one, they pulled themselves up onto the rims and disappeared into the chimney pots in quiet, sooty *ploffs*!

*Ploff! Ploff! Ploff! Ploff!*

Before long, the rooftops of the institute were deserted once more, and the chimneys were gently smoking with faint spirals of disturbed soot. Elliot de Mille was alone at last. He leaned over the low perimeter wall and searched the night sky.

Then, suddenly, they began to arrive. First one, then two, then in a flock – ten pigeons that circled low over the director's head and came to land on the low wall. Elliot de Mille dug into the top pocket of his silk robe and pulled out a handful of bird seed, which he trickled along the wall. The pigeons began pecking greedily at the seed.

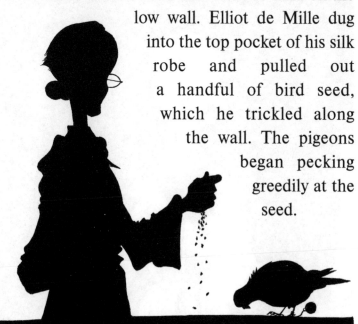

Then, one after the other, Elliot grasped each plump pigeon in a bony hand and gently pulled a small capsule from its leg with the other. He slipped the capsules into his right-hand pocket and released its feathered carrier. When he'd done this to the tenth pigeon, he shooed them all from the wall, and they flapped away over the burnished rooftops and into the dark, black night.

Before turning to go, Elliot smiled his thin smile and patted the top pocket of his monogrammed dressing-gown.

'Thank you, Miss Claw,' he whispered after the departing pigeons. 'You never let me down.'

"Phineas Pepper was an academic explorer too."

# The Compass of the Heart

Once upon a time, there was a young explorer, called Phineas Pepper. Now, one of the interesting things about explorers is that there are lots of different kinds of them.

There are adventuring explorers who like to go to strange far-flung places in search of adventure. This kind of explorer tends to be very rich and turns to exploring because he or she is bored. Theodore Luscombe II, conqueror of Mount Ha-Ha, was one of these.

Then there are commercial explorers. Commercial explorers set off to try and make money from exploring. They usually go in for long sea voyages to distant islands, and some take up useful jobs like bridge-building in far-flung places. A couple of these commercial explorers are quite famous, although you probably won't have heard of them. One is Captain Marcus Crane, who discovered the macadacchio nut, and another is Winthrop Flood, who designed the ill-fated Tamberlaine-Marx Crossing in the Dandoon Delta.

And then there are academic explorers. These explorers neither go off in search of adventure nor deliberately set out to make money – although oddly enough they often end up with plenty of both. Instead, these explorers go travelling to far-flung places in search of knowledge. They love finding out about things and, when they return home, writing all about them in journals and papers and quarterly magazines.

Wilfred McPherson, founder of *The Firefly Quarterly*, was one of these academic explorers. He was a collector of stories, and he travelled all over the world – to the Exotic East, the Sunny South, the Wild West and the Frozen North – in search of them.

Phineas Pepper was an academic explorer too. In fact, he started out as Wilfred McPherson's assistant and worked at the Institute of Travellers' Tales that the story collector had set up in Firefly Square. It was there that he met and fell in love with McPherson's beautiful daughter, Phyllida.

PHYLLIDA PEPPER

They got married and would have lived happily ever after, it hadn't been for one thing.

Phineas was a born explorer. That, after all, is why Phyllida had fallen in love with him, because so was she.

So, when Wilfred McPherson returned from his latest voyage and announced that he was getting too old for exploring and planned to retire and run *The Firefly Quarterly* with help from some friends, Phineas jumped at the chance to take over as chief academic explorer. *He* would travel to far-flung places. *He* would collect the stories from the people he met there, and send them back to his father-in-law, who would publish them in his magazine.

The first thing he did was to order the very latest snow chariot, the *Mark II* from *Crane and Sons*, and set about making plans for a voyage to the Frozen North. And his wife, Phyllida Pepper (who was not only a born explorer, but also extremely headstrong) insisted on coming along too. There was just one problem.

Phyllida was going to have a baby.

So, Phineas postponed the voyage and took on an assistant of his own – a promising engineer called Edward Evesham. Edward had left *Crane and Sons* under a cloud, but he was a wonderful inventor and soon set about making all sorts of ingenious improvements to Phineas and Phyllida's new snow chariot. He strengthened the bump-resistant skis, rebuilt the steam engine and added a bigger propeller. But most ingeniously of all, Edward added a new invention that was all his own. He called it 'The Compass of the Heart'.

At *Crane and Sons*, Edward had worked on all sorts of inventions that you probably have never heard of. One of these inventions was an ingenious little flying box which he designed to send messages over long distances. Well, a lot of the inner workings of Edward's 'Compass of the Heart' were improvements on  those of the flying box – with some mechanical wizardry thrown in for good measure.

The compass could guide you to the four corners of the world without you once having to look at a map or consult a chart. But, more magical than that, it could also guide you back home again – the place which, as everyone knows, is where the heart is.

It was Edward Evesham's greatest invention, and Phineas and Phyllida Pepper were delighted with it. So delighted, in fact, that when Phyllida had a baby boy, they asked Edward Evesham to be his wizard godfather.

BABY HUGO

Six months later, Phineas, Phyllida and baby Hugo set off on a voyage, the destination needle of the 'Compass of the Heart' set on 'The Frozen North'. Their friends had begged them not to go, but Phineas Pepper had simply patted the snow chariot and said, 'With Edward's marvellous improvements, what can possibly go wrong?'

# Chapter Eight

---

## Cosgrove & Cosgrove
### ACCOUNTANT

*1, Montmorency Mews*
*Harbour Heights*

**Re:** Dalle and Daughter Rug Restorers
Account for Previous Four Months

**INCOME** . . . . . . . . . . . . *Nil*

**EXPENSES**
Wool . . . . . . . . . . . . . . . *20 crowns*
Darning Needles . . . . . . . . *8 crowns*
Rent . . . . . . . . . . . . . . . *50 crowns*
Moth-dog biscuits . . . . . . . *1/2 crown*

---

o ahead, Hugo, dear,' said Lily Neptune, pushing open the small door cut into the large double doors of *Evesham's Workshop*. 'He's waiting for you.'

'We won't come in,' said Daisy, taking her sister's arm. 'After all, we've got so many things to do. Pick up the cake, wash our best teacups, prepare the fishing floats – we must have fishing floats, Lily, dear . . .'

'Yes, yes,' said Lily, swishing off down the pavement with her sister. 'But if we don't get on, there won't be time for our afternoon swim.'

'Don't you and Edward be late now, Hugo, dear,' called Daisy as she and her sister disappeared down Brimstone Alley.

Hugo took a deep breath and stepped inside. The workshop was large and spacious, and smelled of oily rags and turpentine. There was a huge skylight high above his head, almost the length and breadth of the roof, which allowed the light to come flooding in.

Despite this, the first thing Hugo noticed was that there were lamps everywhere. Tall angular lamps with swivel-shades, small squat lamps set on scuttling legs, lamps that dimmed and glowed as he approached them, and lamps that followed him when he moved, craning their metallic necks after him like a flock of inquisitive goslings . . .

The next thing Hugo noticed was the snow chariot.

It was suspended from the rafters on heavy metal chains. Hugo approached it through the crowd of lamps – which parted to let him through – and looked up. A tall thin man in an oil-stained apron and carpet slippers of an unusual design stood in mid-air, a long metallic tool in his hand, like a wand.

He was using this to make adjustments to the small propeller at the back of the snow chariot.

*Clink! Clunk! Clink!*

When he caught sight of Hugo looking up at him, Edward Evesham stopped what he was doing and clicked his heels together. Gracefully descending to the floor, he wiped an oily hand on his apron and held it out.

'Hugo! My dear, dear boy!' he exclaimed in a thin, reedy voice. 'I can't tell you how much it means to me to see you again after all these years!'

Hugo shook Edward Evesham's hand.

'Why, the last time I saw you, you were a little baby in your mother's arms . . . Your poor, *dear* mother . . . And your father . . .'

Edward let go of Hugo's hand and turned away, his shoulders hunched. He searched the pockets of his oil-stained apron, pulled out an equally oil-stained handkerchief and blew his nose. Then he turned back to Hugo and cleared his throat.

'Daisy and Lily told me your story, Hugo. We're a close-knit little community here on the south side. We have to be – especially with the institute the way it is these days.'

'Institute?' said Hugo.

'Once upon a time, the institute was a marvellous place,' he said wistfully. 'It published a beautiful magazine, *The Firefly Quarterly*, which was full of fascinating stories collected from far and wide.' Edward Evesham shook his

head. 'But that bounder Elliot de Mille runs the institute now. Mysterious character. Keeps himself to himself. We never see him. All I know is he's turned the *Quarterly* into the nasty, gossip-filled magazine it is today. But enough of all that . . .'

He took Hugo's arm and led him over to a work bench, where he motioned for him to sit down.

'It was a bit of a shock seeing the old *Mark II* chariot after all these years, I must say. Battered and bruised . . .' He paused. 'Then again, the old girl's not in bad shape considering the crash you had.'

'I don't remember too much about it,' said Hugo, squinting through the glare of several inquisitive reading lamps. 'I turned the needle of the compass to *Home* and the chariot seemed to do the rest. We flew for days and days . . . I don't know for how long. I was cold and hungry, but I didn't give up. I gritted my teeth and clung on tightly as the snow chariot flew on and on . . . And then the engine just seemed to cut out and I found myself here.'

'You've been very brave, my boy,' said Edward Evesham, patting Hugo on the shoulder. 'You're an explorer at heart, just like your father, Phineas . . .'

He took out the handkerchief and blew his nose again. Hugo looked down at his feet and swallowed hard.

'I've seen the polar bear claw marks on the chariot,' said Edward sadly. 'Terrible, terrible tragedy.

But at least they didn't get *you* – and of course you've come back to tell us your story. It was the not knowing that was the truly terrible part . . .'

Hugo nodded. Edward sat down beside him.

'If only your grandfather had known the whole story,' he said thoughtfully. 'Perhaps things might have turned out differently.'

'My grandfather?' said Hugo, looking up.

". . . snowmen are extremely shy creatures and
hardly anyone has ever seen one."

# The Story Collector and the Snowmen

Once upon a time, there was a small tribe of snowmen living in the ice forests of the Frozen North. Now, for those of you who don't already know, snowmen are extremely small (only about two feet tall), are covered from head to toe in thick white fur, and have long thin arms and short skinny legs. Their eyes are small and intelligent-looking, their mouths wide and expressive, while their fingers are both long and particularly nimble.

They also have one other feature that is, in many ways, their most remarkable. Snowmen have absolutely enormous feet.

These huge feet have three toes each, which is why you'll also sometimes find snowmen referred to as the three-toed yeti. But not very often, because snowmen are extremely shy creatures and hardly anyone has ever seen one.

What many travellers to the ice forests of the Frozen North *have* seen, however, are the snowmen's footprints. This has quite naturally led them to suppose that the snowmen – or three-toed yeti – are, themselves, absolutely enormous creatures, and has made it seem all the more surprising that nobody has actually seen one.

The other remarkable thing about snowmen, for those of you who don't already know, is that there are hardly any snow-*women*. Snow-women are a little smaller and a lot shyer than snowmen – but they have even bigger feet!

Snowmen spend a lot of their time forlornly wandering through the ice forests looking for the footprints of a snow-woman to follow, in the hope of meeting her. This hardly ever happens and most snowmen live rather sad, solitary lives, brightened up only by the gifts left out for them by superstitious reindeer herders.

But once in a very long while, a snowman will actually meet a small, shy, big-footed snow-woman and, after a good deal of foot thumping and toe wiggling, they'll usually decide to have a family. Now, for those of you who don't already know, a snow-woman doesn't just have one snow-baby at a time.

Or twins. Or even triplets . . . No, she has no fewer than two hundred in one go.

This is probably why snow-women are so shy in the first place.

Now, one snowy day, a snowman was wandering forlornly through the ice forest when he saw a sight to melt his snowy heart. It was an absolutely *enormous* footprint. In fact, a whole line of them. He immediately started following them. They led through the ice forest and into a clearing, where they ended just beside an old *Crane and Sons Aeronautical Snow Chariot - Mark I*. Now the snowman had never seen a *Crane and Sons Aeronautical Snow Chariot - Mark I* before, and to him it looked very strange and rather scary – but having followed the giant footprints this far, he wasn't about to give up now. So he walked up to the snow chariot, sniffed, tasted the air and looked inside.

Just then, the snowman heard footsteps behind him in the snow. What was more, they were approaching. So he did what comes naturally to any snowman.

He hid.

Wilfred McPherson, academic explorer and story collector, appeared a few moments later. Without pausing for a moment, he climbed into the snow chariot – which, after many voyages and adventures was getting rather rickety and unreliable – aligned the skis, adjusted the hot-air balloon and set off for his home, far away in the bustling city of Harbour Heights.

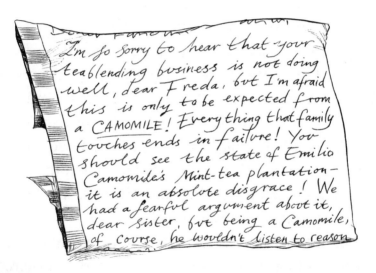

# Chapter Nine

I'm so sorry to hear that your teablending business is not doing well, dear Freda, but I'm afraid this is only to be expected from a CAMOMILE! Everything that family touches ends in failure! You should see the state of Emilio Camomile's Mint-tea plantation—it is an absolute disgrace! We had a fearful argument about it, dear sister, but being a Camomile, of course, he wouldn't listen to reason

The lights of the institute shone through its shuttered windows, behind which came the measured and rhythmical *clackety-clack* of well-oiled printing presses. In his large office, Elliot de Mille turned from the white-washed oval window, with its spy-holes, and crossed to the large black blind that hung from the opposite wall.

The director of the institute wore a large green visor, a spotless printer's apron and black detachable sleeves over his crisp white shirt. Reaching down, Elliot tugged on the cord attached to the bottom of the blind, which snapped up, to reveal the glass wall behind.

Elliot de Mille took the propelling pencil from behind his ear and began tapping it against his front teeth in time to the *clackety-clack* of the printing presses as he looked down at the view through the wall of glass. His thin lips stretched into a pinched smile.

'That's what I like to see,' he muttered. 'Busy activity to bring the latest revelations about their city to the good people of Harbour Heights.' He hissed with amusement. '*And* the bad.'

Below him lay a large, cavernous hall in which four great printing presses were hard at work. Clustered round them with oil cans, spanners, sponges and tubs of printer's ink were dozens of small furry creatures, each wearing green visors. Beyond them, dozens more were busy unrolling large sheets of paper and feeding them to the presses, while still more were

operating a giant guillotine that chopped the printed sheets into pages ready for binding. Large pendulous lamps hung from the roof beams, bathing the whole scene in a golden light as the creatures padded backwards and forwards on their huge sooty feet.

There was a soft knock on the office door. Elliot turned from the glass wall.

'Enter!' he barked.

A small furry creature in a green visor entered and handed the director a freshly printed copy of *The Firefly Quarterly*, which he snatched greedily.

'You may go,' he said, 'but if I find any errors, you can tell them from me, there'll be no foot-cooling for a week!'

The creature nodded and padded out of the room.

Elliot settled himself in his big swivel-chair, put his feet up on his enormous desk and was just about to begin reading when he became aware of an uncomfortable sensation – that of being watched.

He looked up. Two hundred pairs of small eyes were staring intently back at him from beneath green visors. Elliot put down the magazine and crossed to the glass wall.

'Get back to work!' he barked, before yanking the black blind down again.

Settling once more in his chair, Elliot de Mille flicked through the pages of *The Firefly Quarterly,* article after article dripping with syrupy words of praise for those people and businesses with secrets to hide, who had made generous donations. Other pages were full of tittle-tattle, scandal and rumour, all designed to encourage others to do the same.

Elliot de Mille smiled his thin smile.

Stealing secrets and selling stories . . . He loved it! It made him feel important and powerful, and so much cleverer than everybody else. Indeed, his life would have been perfect, but for one thing – he could never step foot outside the institute for fear of being recognized by those busybodies on the south side of the square. So long as they remained in their poky little shops, his own secret would never be safe. If it got out, then he wouldn't feel important or powerful or cleverer than everybody else. Instead, he would feel small and vulnerable and despised, just as he once had.

And he, Elliot de Mille wasn't about to let that happen.

He got up and crossed to the oval window, and looked out of the spy-holes at the shops on the south side of Firefly Square.

'Soon,' he whispered, 'Firefly Square will all be mine.'

"Alfie Spangle hated that bicycle."

# The Firefly Quarterly

*O*nce upon a time, there was a young butcher's boy called Alfie Spangle. His job was to deliver his father's sausages (considered by many to be the very best in bustling Harbour Heights) to every part of the town, on a bicycle that had a large wheel at the back and a small wheel at the front. The bicycle also had a big wicker basket attached to the handlebars in which to put the sausages.

Alfie Spangle hated that bicycle. It was slow, it was heavy and it was difficult to pedal – especially on the steep hills which led up to the large squares of the Heights. But most of all, Alfie hated the bicycle because the children in those squares – who had expensive shiny bicycles without baskets and with wheels of the same size – used to make fun of him for having to ride it.

Children, for those of you who don't already know, can be cruel, and the rich children with their expensive bicycles were crueller than most when it came to Alfie Spangle, the butcher's boy. Many was the time that, having finished his deliveries to the Heights, Alfie would set off for Firefly Square, feeling stupid and hopeless and insignificant.

Firefly Square, which was small and often overlooked, was where Alfie made his final deliveries of the day, taking those remaining parcels of sausages in his basket to the strange shops on the south side. The thing was, by the time Alfie got to Firefly Square he would nearly always be in a filthy temper, hating the whole of Harbour Heights and everyone in it. All he wanted to do was fling those last sausages down onto the steps of *Evesham's Workshop* or *Camomile and Camomile* and slink off to the gardens, where he would throw his hated bicycle down in front of the odd little fountain with its sculpture of a one-eared cat, and sulk.

Unfortunately for Alfie Spangle, the shopkeepers of the south side of Firefly Square were simply too friendly to let that happen. For instance, whenever either of the two Miss Neptunes saw the sullen young butcher's boy, they would always say hello and ask after his father.

But Alfie wasn't fooled. He knew they didn't mean it, and he hated them for being so cheerful – just as much as he hated those creepy Camomiles, who offered him cups of tea out of pity, and that stupid Edward Evesham, who was only making fun of him when he offered to improve his bicycle. And as for the Dalles, they had suggested he wear a pair of carpet slippers which they claimed would help him pedal his bicycle.

Carpet slippers! Did they think he was stupid? They were all, Alfie Spangle decided, even crueller than the children in Montmorency Square.

The only person young Alfie *didn't* hate was someone he met by the fountain one day in the gardens of Firefly Square. She was tatty, and odd, and surrounded by thin yellow alley cats. What was more, she seemed almost as miserable and bitter as he was.

Now, since Alfie was a butcher's boy who delivered sausages on a slow, heavy bicycle, it wasn't surprising that he was always being chased by dogs. Big dogs, small dogs; dogs that jumped at his sausage basket barking loudly. Once he'd been knocked off his bicycle by a pack of greedy poodles who had eaten the lot. For this and other indignities, Alfie Spangle hated dogs almost as much as he hated people. So it seemed natural for him to like cats – especially those thin, dirty alley cats who also hated dogs.

Cressida Claw and her cats befriended Alfie, and together they talked about all the people they hated in Harbour Heights. They had a lot in common.

Then one day, Mr Spangle senior sold his sausage shop to Bernard Bumble, the meat-pie magnate, and moved to the Sunny South, and Alfie – who was by now far too old to be a butcher's boy – was left wondering what to do with the rest of his life.

As luck would have it, it was just then that Cressida Claw discovered that Wilfred McPherson of the Institute of Travellers' Tales was looking for a new assistant. His old one had apparently disappeared on an intrepid voyage to the Frozen North.

Not long afterwards, a young man in a cheap, ill-fitting suit and slicked-back hair appeared at the Institute and introduced himself as Elliot de Mille, a brilliant young expert in nautical yarns and sea-shanties. Wilfred McPherson had become a recluse after the disappearance of his daughter and son-in-law and had even lost interest in the institute's journal, *The Firefly Quarterly*. The young man seemed keen and came bearing a long list of impeccable qualifications, so without any further ado, the story collector took him on as his assistant on a four-month trial.

Time passed, Wilfred McPherson moved to the Sunny South - according to Elliot de Mille, who became the institute's new director - and the institute began to change . . .

Shutters went up at its windows, visiting scholars and interested members of the public were turned away, and its doors - previously open - were locked. In fact nobody was seen to enter or to leave.

Once every four months, delivery boys on butchers' bicycles, hired from Bernard Bumble, would arrive and load their baskets with bundles of *The Firefly Quarterly* which were waiting for them in stacks outside the institute. These they'd deliver to the squares and streets of Harbour Heights, where anxious-looking, tight-lipped people would be waiting to read the contents.

Schoolboys who had misbehaved, worried actors wearing false beards and meat-pie magnates with something to hide scoured the contents of *The Firefly Quarterly*, hoping that their donations were large enough to stop their secrets being revealed. How on earth, they often wondered, had the *Quarterly*

discovered these secrets? Nobody knew, yet issue after issue was full of gossip and tittle-tattle of the worst sort.

More time passed, and most people forgot – as people are liable to do – that the magazine had ever been any different. Most people, that is, except for the residents of Firefly Square.

# Chapter Ten

Craddock's Nuts & Bolts
12b Herring Walk
Harbour Heights

Dear Mr Evesham,

The firm of Craddock's Nuts & Bolts must regretfully decline to supply you with any further goods until all outstanding debts with this firm are settled in full.

Yours faithfully,

*Ambrose Craddock*

h, there you are, Hugo! And Edward, I see,' smiled Daisy Neptune, opening the door of *Dalle and Daughter*. 'Right on time. Everyone's here.'

Hugo stared at her. She was wearing a stunning necklace of pearls, eight strings long, and two large dangling coral earrings. Her green spectacles gleamed and her bronze-coloured hair tumbled down over her shoulders in a great cascade of auburn curls.

Hugo and Edward Evesham – who had taken off his apron and put on a shiny black frock-coat – stepped into the carpet shop. Tik-Tik climbed off his cushion and gave a short, dusty bark, then spotted a moth and disappeared after it.

'Come through, come through!' trilled Daisy excitedly, swishing past the heavy hanging carpets.

At the entrance to the back room, they were greeted by an equally excited Lily. She was dressed similarly to her sister, but wore a shark-tooth tiara and carried a trident studded with sea shells.

'Look what we've done with the place!' she beamed.

Hugo gasped.

Meena Dalle's back room was bedecked with glass fishing floats, hanging in great clusters from the ceiling high above. Each float glowed, lit from within by a candle of sweet-scented sea lavender. Hovering in mid-air amidst the flickering constellation was a circle of flying carpets, each with an embroidered cushion upon it. Freda and Diego Camomile were sitting on one, and pouring cups of tea. Meena sat on another.

Looking down, she smiled and, with a click of her fingers, sent three others gently wafting down to the floor. Daisy and Lily settled themselves onto the first, Edward Evesham climbed onto the middle one. Hugo set himself gingerly down on the third rug, which rose gently to join the others in mid-air.

'"Fond Farewell" tea,' said Diego, handing a cup to Hugo.

'So you've heard,' said Hugo.

'We all have, dear Hugo,' said Meena in her musical voice.

'It's just that I had to find out where *Home* on the compass was,' said Hugo, 'because I knew that that must be the place my parents came from – the place where I was born. And it's been amazing to see Firefly Square and to meet all of you, who were their friends, and who cared about them. But this isn't *my* home . . .' he said, tears in his eyes.

'Hugo misses his parents, Harvi and Sarvi, and is anxious to get back to them,' interrupted Edward Evesham. 'We had a long chat about it this afternoon, didn't we, Hugo, lad?'

Hugo nodded.

'The snow chariot is fully repaired,' he went on, 'packed with provisions and on my roof ready for launch, whenever you are, my boy. I've re-calibrated the Compass of the Heart, so the old girl should get you back to Harvi and Sarvi safe and sound.'

'It will?' said Hugo. 'That's fantastic!'

'Yes, quite simple really,' said Edward Evesham. 'A little bit of mechanical wizardry. *Home* is now where *your* heart is; in the Frozen North.' The old inventor beamed. 'And should you wish to, Hugo, my boy, you can return and visit us all again, just by turning the dial to Firefly Square. But next time, be sure to pack enough cheese!'

Hugo smiled and wiped his eyes.

'Well, if that's settled,' said Daisy brightly, her eyes glistening moistly behind her green spectacles. 'Let's have some cake!'

Lily produced a beautifully decorated seedcake which filled the room with the smell of honey and toasted sesame, and handed round slices. Everyone tried to sound jolly and cheerful, but Hugo could see that he reminded them so much of his parents

– the parents that he had never known – that they all seemed lost in their own thoughts . . .

Memories of Phineas and Phyllida Pepper. And the old days when Firefly Square had been a happy place – a time before his parents had left, and his grandfather had disappeared to the Sunny South; a time before the institute shuttered its windows and locked its doors and the mysterious Elliot de Mille had taken over *The Firefly Quarterly* to spread malicious gossip and harmful rumour.

Despite the beautiful floats and the magical carpets, the delicious tea and rich buttery cake, Hugo felt sad and homesick for the Frozen North. At last – after seemingly endless stories about his grandfather and how each of them had first found their way to Firefly Square – it was time for bed, and Hugo said his thank-yous and goodbyes.

Meena insisted that he take the seedcake – which had hardly been touched – and put it back in the Fateful Voyage Bakery box. Then he walked the two doors along the road to *Neptune's Nautical Antiques*, said goodnight to Edward Evesham and followed Daisy and Lily up the stairs of the little shop.

Back in his bedroom, he opened the box and took out a piece of seedcake. Then he crossed to the window, opened it and placed the slice on the window sill, gazing out at Firefly Square in the moonlight for the last time.

'For the snow giants,' he said, with a smile.

# Part Two

# The Firefly Quarterly

Nº 1

## THE SWAMP VOLE AND THE LONGBILL AND OTHER FABLES

# MYTHS OF THE DANDOON DELTA

ISSUE

THE FIREFLY QUARTERLY · JOURNAL OF THE INSTITUTE OF TRAVELLERS' TALES.
· EDITOR : WILFRED McPHERSON ·

# Chapter Eleven

Hugo dreamed that the beautiful sea-bed had sprouted real branches with glistening, dew-soaked leaves and luscious fruit, all ripe for the picking. He climbed up into the branches and reached out to grasp a bunch of blackcurrants, which turned to Archduke Ferdinand's Florentines the moment he touched them.

Diego Camomile leaned down and offered him a cup of *Fond Farewell* tea, which seemed to taste of sea water. Daisy and Lily Neptune swam past, pursued by a toothless shark, and Meena Dalle offered him a pair of slippers, while Edward Evesham – dressed in a bird suit – tapped out a tune on the branches of the sea-bed with a wizard's wand.

Hugo put the slippers on – and found they were made of seedcake. Edward seemed to be trying to tell him something, but the Camomiles were twittering in one ear and Meena was cooing in the other, and Edward turned into a seagull and started squawking and flapping and pecking at Hugo's seedcake slippers . . .

Hugo opened his eyes. A large seagull was perched on the curling wrought iron at the foot of the sea-bed. It let out a loud squawk and flapped its wings noisily.

Hugo sat up. The sea-bed was full of roosting birds. There were several blue starlings with bright yellow eyes, at least five dusty-looking sparrows, a pair of seagulls and, perched just above his pillow, a plump pigeon. His bedroom window was open, but the shutters had blown shut, and the torn, shredded remains of the Fateful Voyage cake box lay on the bedspread at his feet.

There was not a single piece of seedcake to be seen, however, not even a crumb. The seagulls squawked again as Hugo climbed sleepily out of bed and went over to the window.

So much for leaving seedcake on the window sill, he thought. The ways of the Frozen North didn't quite fit down here in Harbour Heights.

Hugo pushed the window shutters open and shooed the disgruntled seagulls and their companions out. The sparrows flapped about against the ceiling light and one starling upset the upright lamp in the corner – but in the end Hugo managed to get all the birds out. All, that is, except for the plump pigeon, which sat contentedly on its perch on a wrought-iron branch of the sea-bed. It regarded him with one quizzical eye; then the other.

'Come on, you stupid thing!' Hugo tutted irritably. 'There's no more seedcake, if that's what you're after.'

But the pigeon didn't move. It just put its head to one side and cooed softly. Then Hugo saw it. A small, metallic capsule attached by a ring to the bird's left leg. It seemed to have a little catch on its side, like the ones you find on a bracelet or a string of pearls. Hugo leaned forwards and gently released the capsule by flicking back the catch. It fell into the palm of his hand. The pigeon shifted on to its other leg and observed him with one eye.

The capsule had a seam round the middle, and Hugo carefully twisted it using both hands. It unscrewed, and inside he found a piece of paper which had been neatly folded into a small square. Intrigued, Hugo unfolded it and read the spidery scrawl on the headed notepaper:

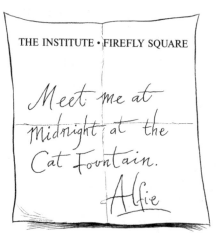

THE INSTITUTE · FIREFLY SQUARE

*Meet me at Midnight at the Cat Fountain.*

*Alfie*

The institute? The mysterious institute with its shuttered windows and locked doors that he'd heard so much about? The institute which produced that horrible gossipy magazine? Hugo felt butterflies fluttering in the pit of his stomach. This message was obviously not meant for his eyes. It was the seedcake that had been responsible for bringing it to him.

So who *was* it meant for? he wondered. There was only one way to find out.

Hugo folded the paper up again, returned it to the little capsule and attached it to the ring on the pigeon's leg. Then he picked up the plump bird and crossed to the open window. The sun was rising over the rooftops of Firefly Square as Hugo stretched his arms out of the window and released the pigeon, which flapped away with its mysterious message, carrying it to the person for whom it was intended.

The snow chariot was ready and waiting for him on the roof of Edward Evesham's workshop, but his departure could wait another day, Hugo told himself. He gazed out across Firefly Gardens at the institute opposite, his curiosity getting the better of him.

'Midnight,' he whispered.

# The Firefly Quarterly

Nº 12

THE
SHEPHERDESS
WHO
TOUCHED THE
MOON

# FOLKTALES OF THE RANDOO KUSH

ISSUE

· JOURNAL OF THE INSTITUTE OF TRAVELLERS' TALES ·

EDITOR · WILFRED McPHERSON

# Chapter Twelve

reakfast, Hugo, dear,' Daisy called from downstairs. 'Grilled sardines, fresh from the harbour this morning!'

Hugo closed his window, hurriedly dressed in the stripy vest, canvas trousers and over-sized sailor's jacket – leaving the sou'wester on the chair by his sea-bed – and clattered down the stairs.

'Why, Hugo, dear,' said Lily, who was drying her long bronze-coloured hair beside the ship's galley stove in the corner of the cluttered kitchen. 'I put out your reindeer herder clothes for you. After all, I thought–'

'*I* thought I might just stay a little bit longer,' Hugo interrupted, sitting down at the large barrel that served as a kitchen table. 'I mean, if that's all right with you and Daisy.'

'Of course it is!' exclaimed Daisy, swishing over with a plate of grilled sardines and seaweed toast. 'As long as we've still got a roof over our heads, you'll be welcome under it, Hugo, dear.'

The Neptune sisters smiled at Hugo as he helped himself to a sardine and a piece of seaweed toast.

'There's something I'd like to ask you,' said Hugo, taking a sip of Camomiles' *Sunny Morning* tea. 'Do either of you know anybody by the name of Alfie?'

'Alfie?' said Lily, finishing drying her hair and swishing over to join Daisy and Hugo at the table. 'Alfie . . . Alfie . . . The name does seem familiar. There was an Alfred Ampleside who had a small tug-boat. Freddie Fishface, we used to call him . . .'

'Or that butcher's boy, Lily, dear,' said Daisy. 'Always miserable. Had a face like a storm at sea. *His* name was Alfie.'

'So it was!' exclaimed Lily, gazing at her sister through her green spectacles. 'Alfie Spangle.'

'Does he work at the institute?' asked Hugo, intrigued.

'Little Alfie Spangle?' exclaimed Daisy, laughing. 'Of course not, dear. His father, old Sid Spangle, sold his sausage shop and moved to the Sunny South years ago, and that's the last we ever saw of Alfie and that funny old bicycle of his.'

'Alfie Spangle working at the institute,' Lily giggled. 'Whatever gave you that idea, Hugo, dear?'

But before Hugo could answer, a copy of *The Firefly Quarterly* came through the letterbox and landed with a thump on the seagrass welcome-mat. Lily and Daisy stopped laughing and exchanged worried looks.

After breakfast, Hugo left the Neptune sisters *tut-tutting* and shaking their heads over *The Firefly Quarterly* and visited *Dalle and Daughter: Rug Restorers*.

Tik-Tik the moth-dog jumped off his cushion and came trotting over to lick his hand. Hugo tickled him behind the ears, then brushed past the hanging carpets and entered the back room.

Meena was hovering in mid-air in her flying carpet slippers, darning a battered looking carpet that was stretched in the frame on the far wall. As Hugo entered, she turned and smiled. Then, with a click of her heels, she sank to the ground and gave him a fierce hug.

'Hugo! Darling boy!' she exclaimed in her musical voice. 'I thought you were leaving first thing this morning.'

'I was,' said Hugo, 'but when I woke up . . . well, I thought I'd stay just a little bit longer.'

'Stay as long as you like, Hugo. It's so lovely having you here with us.'

'Meena,' said Hugo, when she'd released him from the hug. 'Where is the cat fountain?'

'You mean you didn't see it when you arrived?' said Meena. She looked surprised, then thoughtful. 'Though I suppose you did rather crash-land, didn't you? Thank goodness for the flying carpet.'

'I don't remember much about it, to be honest,' said Hugo, shaking his head. 'Just falling and then, instead of hitting the ground with a thump, I seemed to land so softly . . .'

'In a tree not far from the old fountain in the middle of Firefly Square,' said Meena, smiling. 'It has a small statue of a one-eared ship's cat called Treacle on it.'

'So *that's* the cat fountain,' said Hugo thoughtfully.

But Meena didn't reply. She was looking with a worried expression at the copy of *The Firefly Quarterly* which Tik-Tik had just dropped at her feet.

Hugo didn't stay long at Meena Dalle's. She seemed distracted and worried, and kept picking up and putting down *The Firefly Quarterly* as if she couldn't quite bring herself to open it and look inside. Instead, he went next door to *Camomile and Camomile: Tea Blenders*.

There, he found Diego on the landing at the top of the spiral staircase. He had a set of small scales in front of him and was wearing a waistcoat with dozens of small pockets, each one containing a teaspoon of a different size. On the small fold-up table beside him were several large tins of tea with labels on them such as *Quick-Witted Blue Bush*, *Bold and Brave Broadleaf* and *Delicious Irony Mint*. Diego dipped into these tins with one or other of the teaspoons from his waistcoat and sprinkled their contents into the left- or right-hand pan of the scales – which, Hugo realized on closer inspection, were in fact miniature teapots, each being warmed from beneath by a candle.

'Just a new blend I'm working on, Hugo, my boy,' smiled Diego when he saw the fascinated expression on Hugo's face. 'Thought I'd call it Camomile's *Lionheart* tea. What do you think?'

'It sounds wonderful,' said Hugo, bending down to examine the scales. 'Diego, do you know anybody called Alfie who works for the institute?'

'Alfie? At the institute?' Diego took a teaspoon from his waistcoat and tapped it thoughtfully against a tin marked *Dandoon Derring-do*. 'No,' he said at last, 'I can't say as I do. The institute pokes into everyone else's business, but when it comes to its own, it's as secretive as a blue monkey's tea party. Now, it was different in your grandfather's day . . .'

Just then, Freda Camomile's voice came floating up from the basement.

'Diego, dear, that beastly *Firefly Quarterly* has arrived, but I can't bear to open it. I feel faint, Diego, and my heart's all a-flutter!'

After lunch, Hugo left the Camomiles and popped his head round the door of *Evesham's Workshop*.

'Leaving it rather late, my lad,' said Edward

Evesham, putting down the angle-poise lamp he was adjusting and wiping his hands on his apron. 'The old girl's packed and waiting – but it's mid-afternoon. I thought you were making an early start this morning.'

'I was,' said Hugo, 'but I changed my mind. Tomorrow morning, perhaps . . .'

'Excellent stuff! Delighted to have you around,' said Edward, turning the lamp on and directing its light onto his workbench. Hugo saw a copy of *The Firefly Quarterly* lying open next to an oil can.

'Nobody seems to like *The Firefly Quarterly*,' said Hugo, picking it up and flicking through its pages, 'and yet everybody seems to read it . . .'

Edward shook his head and took the copy from Hugo. He turned to the back page.

'That, Hugo, my lad, is because it's full of rumours and tittle-tattle and untrue stories, and everybody is afraid that they'll be in it. That's the reason they're always making donations to it – so *The Firefly Quarterly* won't say anything nasty about them.'

'Do *you* make donations?' asked Hugo.

Edward didn't reply. Instead, he just smiled

ruefully and pointed to the back page. Hugo read the article there.

# SOUTHSIDE SHOPKEEPERS STRAPPED FOR CASH

It has come to the Quarterly's notice that the peculiar little shops on the south side of Firefly Square are more than usually rundown and empty of customers.

Not surprising, you might think, given their reputation for shoddy workmanship, over-priced harbour junk and sawdust-filled tea.

But not for much longer! The Quarterly has it on good authority that the money has run out for the shoddy shopkeepers, and change is in the air in Firefly Square!

*The Firefly Quarterly, Page 47*

'What do *you* think? said Edward Evesham, shaking his head.

# The Firefly Quarterly

Nº 29

THE BLUE MONKEYS'
TEA PARTY
AND
OTHER STORIES FROM THE JUNGLE

TALL TALES FROM THE SUNNY SOUTH

ISSUE

JOURNAL OF THE INSTITUTE OF TRAVELLERS' TALES .
EDITOR: WILFRED McPHERSON · ASSIST. EDITOR: E. de MILLE ·

# Chapter Thirteen

ugo wrapped the blanket round his shoulders and climbed the tall tree in the corner of the gardens of Firefly Square.

He found a branch about halfway up, and settled down to wait. Peering through the leaves, he had a perfect view of the small fountain in the centre of the gardens.

It wasn't surprising that he'd overlooked it before, he thought. Not only was the little park neglected and overgrown, but the fountain's stone base - carved into a scallop shell resting on a mossy plinth - was half covered in ivy.

Water had once filled the shell, but now, apart from a couple of old fish bones and a pebble or two, it was dry and empty. At the centre of the fountain was a carved stone pillar from which two rusty iron seagulls protruded. Their beaks, which must once have acted as decorative water spouts, had long since dried up. On top of the pillar sat a small sculpture of a thin, one-eared cat, clasping a curled scroll in its front paws. From his look-out point in the branches of the tree, Hugo could just make out the words *Treacle – The Ship's Cat* inscribed on the scroll.

It was half-past eleven by the old ship's clock in the window of *Neptune's Nautical Antiques* when Hugo had tip-toed out and quietly closed the door behind him. The Neptune sisters had been quiet and subdued all evening, and had gone up early to bed. They'd clearly been upset by *The Firefly Quarterly* and Hugo didn't want to bother them with stories of pigeons carrying messages – which he shouldn't have been reading in the first place.

Then again, he was glad that he had. And as he sat perfectly still in the branches of the very tree he'd

crashed into only a few nights earlier, he couldn't help wondering who he might see in the gardens beneath him at midnight.

He didn't have much longer to wait.

Down below, treading nimbly in soft mouse-skin boots, came an elderly woman in a shabby coat and a patched and ragged skirt. Her large-brimmed hat of velveteen was held in place with several hat pins and was decorated with a long silver fish bone. In one hand she clutched a cat-head umbrella, and over one arm was slung an enormous leather handbag, as big as a suitcase. Her large, deep-sunken eyes were ringed in dark blue and on her upper lip, several long silvery whiskers quivered as she peered around her.

Then – apparently satisfied that the gardens were deserted – the woman stretched her scraggy neck forward, opened her mouth and gave a thin, piercing *miaooww!*

As if in answer, from the dark clumps of the bushes and shadows beneath the trees, a dozen miaowing calls sounded. One by one, thin scruffy yellow cats slunk out on to the overgrown path and circled the fountain. As they approached the old woman they

dropped the crumpled pieces of
paper they were carrying in
their jaws at her feet,
like proud house-cats
dropping sparrows on
a sitting-room rug.

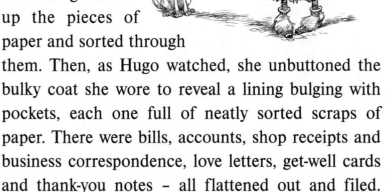

With a greedy
glint in her eyes
and her whiskers
quivering, the old
woman gathered
up the pieces of
paper and sorted through
them. Then, as Hugo watched, she unbuttoned the
bulky coat she wore to reveal a lining bulging with
pockets, each one full of neatly sorted scraps of
paper. There were bills, accounts, shop receipts and
business correspondence, love letters, get-well cards
and thank-you notes – all flattened out and filed.
Besides the bulging paper-filled pockets, there was
something else that caught Hugo's eye.

It was a row of metallic capsules – just like the
one he'd discovered on the plump pigeon in his

bedroom – hanging from small fish-hooks stitched into the lining of the coat. For a few moments, the woman slipped each piece of paper into various pockets, crooning softly to herself while the cats waited patiently, staring at her with unblinking yellow eyes. When she had finished, she buttoned up her coat, set down the enormous handbag and opened it wide.

Inside was a row of pigeon-holes, each one containing a plump cooing pigeon. The old lady ignored them, and instead pulled a greasy grey sack from the depths of the bag before snapping it shut again.

'Here you are, my darlings,' she crooned to the waiting cats, dipping into the sack and pulling out a handful of pungent fish-heads. 'Mummy hasn't forgotten you. See? Mummy loves her beautiful clever catty-kins . . .'

Each cat leaped up to take a fish-head in mid-air as the old woman swept her arm in a wide arc and let the handful go. Then, gripping their pungent suppers delicately in their jaws, they slunk back, silently, into the shadows.

Just then, a tall angular man with a mean pinched-looking face and small shifty eyes stepped out of the bushes and approached the fountain. He had a thin moustache and wire spectacles, and was wearing a long expensive-looking black overcoat and a tall black silk hat. He carried a gold-tipped ebony cane and had on soft kid gloves of duck-egg blue.

'Well, well, ain't you a sight for sore eyes, Alfie, love,' said the old lady, with a wheezy, cackling laugh. 'You gets grander every time we meet. Just like them folks in Montmorency Square, and no mistake!'

'They don't seem so grand when you know all their dirty little secrets, now do they, Cressida?' smiled the tall thin man, adjusting his silk tie and tipping his hat to the cat lady.

'Indeed, they don't, Alfie, love,' Cressida Claw cackled. 'Indeed they don't. Not half as grand as Alfie Spangle – or should I say, Elliot de Mille, Esquire.'

The director of the institute joined in with the cat woman's laughter. In the tree above, Hugo sat very still indeed, while from surrounding bushes there came the sound of fish-heads being crunched.

'Always a pleasure to see you, Cressida, old friend. You've stuck by me through thick and thin, right from the very beginning.' Elliot de Mille, the director of the institute, shivered with distaste as he remembered his life as young Alfie Spangle the butcher's boy. 'Which is why I had to tell you the news in person!'

'The news, Alfie, love?' said Cressida, her dark-rimmed eyes growing wide and her whiskers quivering. 'What news?'

'What would you say to a great big pigeon loft, and a cattery, and a place to call your very own, Cressida, old friend?' Elliot de Mille smirked delightedly.

'Now, if I've told you once, I've told you a thousand times, Alfie, love,' said Cressida Claw, frowning and crossing her arms. 'I'm not moving into that institute of yours; not with all those nasty stumpy big-footed little horrors. Worse than dogs, if you ask me – and you know how I feel about dogs, Alfie, love . . .'

Elliot de Mille gave a shrill, cackling laugh. 'No, not the institute, Cressida. I know you won't go near it. But how about a step up from the back alleys of Harbour Heights? How about Firefly Square?'

'But where, Alfie, love?' said Cressida suspiciously.

'The *south* side!' announced Elliot de Mille with a wave of his ebony cane.

'What, a little shop?' said Cressida, her whiskers twitching uncontrollably. 'Which one, Alfie, love? Which one?'

Elliot de Mille puffed out his thin chest proudly. 'All of them!' he said.

# The Firefly Quarterly

Nº 47

SNOW GIANTS OF THE ICE FORESTS

# FIRESIDE STORIES FROM THE FROZEN NORTH ISSUE

EDITOR :
WILFRED MᶜPHERSON

DIRECTOR
ELLIOT de MILLE

JOURNAL OF THE INSTITUTE OF TRAVELLERS' TALES.

# Chapter Fourteen

As soon as the coast seemed clear, Hugo jumped from the branch of the tree, wrapped in his blanket of cloud sheep wool. As it reached the ground, the blanket hovered and unfurled like a flower opening its petals, and Hugo stepped off it lightly. Pausing only to wrap the blanket around his shoulders, he hurried back through the gardens to the south side of the square.

Quietly, he slipped through the door of *Neptune's Nautical Antiques*, and crept through the cluttered shop and into the kitchen. There, yawning sleepily, he made himself a cup of Camomiles' 'Clear Your Head' tea and sat down with it at the barrel that served as a table. He needed to think.

Clearly Elliot de Mille, or Alfie Spangle or whatever his name was, seemed intent on forcing Hugo's parents' friends out of Firefly Square so that his accomplice – the creepy cat woman – could move in.

Hugo shuddered and took a sip of tea.

She and those cats of hers obviously supplied him with all the information for the nasty stories he printed in that quarterly of his. What a mean trick!

Hugo yawned.

A nasty, mean, deceitful low-down trick! Hugo suddenly felt very homesick for the little cabin in the ice forests of the Frozen North where life was a lot simpler. He put his head in his hands and slumped over the barrel.

I must warn the Neptunes about this Alfie Spangle person . . . *Yawn* . . . First thing . . . *Yawn* . . . in the . . . morning . . .

Hugo was back in the little cabin in front of the glowing stove. Harvi and Sarvi were laughing and singing and telling stories about reindeer and polar bears and snow giants. He was laughing and singing too, and then he began trying to tell them about Firefly Square and the one-eared cat fountain, and

Elliot de Mille. Or Alfie Spangle. He opened and closed his mouth, but no words came out . . .

*Bang! Bang! Bang!*

Hugo snapped awake and sat up. The *Clear Your Head* tea was sitting in front of him, stone cold.

*Bang! Bang! Bang!*

Daisy and Lily Neptune came swishing down the stairs, all a-flutter.

'We're closed, you know,' trilled Daisy.

'We haven't even had our morning swim,' added Lily, peering through the clutter at the shop window.

Hugo jumped up from the barrel and ran through to join them in the shop.

'You're up early, Hugo, dear,' smiled Daisy. 'Perhaps you'd better open the door, Lily, dear. Before whoever it is breaks the knocker.'

Lily slid back the bolts, top and bottom, and opened the door. A small, rather plump gentleman in a grey overcoat and large bowler hat stood holding a clipboard and pen. When he saw Lily and Daisy, he tipped his hat and gave a short, dry little cough.

'*Ahem!* Good morning, Miss Lily and Miss Daisy Neptune? My name's Horace Pingle of Pingle, Pingle, Duff and Pingle, bailiffs acting on behalf of your creditors . . .'

'Bailiffs?' said Daisy.

'Creditors?' said Lily.

'I'm afraid your rent became overdue today – at one minute past midnight to be exact,' said Horace Pingle, 'and the director of the institute has decided to evict you. Please sign here.'

'Evict us!' said Daisy and Lily, both together.

'You have five minutes to collect your personal items. All other goods in the shop will be sold to pay your rent and, *ahem* . . . eviction costs.'

'What eviction costs?' said Hugo, flushing an angry red.

'Well,' said Horace Pingle, blushing himself. 'There's my fee, and the fees of Pingle, Duff and Pingle over there . . . Eviction is a costly business.'

Hugo looked along the pavement. Three other bailiffs were there, one outside each of the other shops on the south side, clipboards in hand. *Bang! Bang! Bang! – Bang! Bang! Bang! – Bang! Bang! Bang!*

180

They knocked on each of the doors in turn.

Five minutes later, a motley group of individuals stood on the pavement on the south side of Firefly Square. Behind them, men in bowler hats were hammering signs reading UNDER NEW MANAGEMENT onto the door of each shop.

'This is all Alfie Spangle's fault,' said Hugo bitterly, clutching his rolled-up blanket and reindeer herder's costume.

'Alfie Spangle?' said Daisy and Lily Neptune.

'The butcher's boy?' said the Camomiles and Edward Evesham.

'Never mind that for the moment,' said Meena Dalle, tearfully. 'What are we going to do right now?'

*Tap-tap-tap!*

All heads turned to see the tall grey figure of the lamplighter come round the corner of Sleeping Horse Lane and walk towards them. He paused and reached up, and put out the lamp on the corner, then moved on.

*Tap-tap-tap!*

The lamplighter stopped and looked at the small group standing beneath the next lamppost with his

watery, grey eyes. He looked at
their suitcases and packing
trunks; he looked at their sad,
shocked faces; he looked at Hugo
Pepper, small and defiant,
in his sou'wester and
oversized sailor's jacket
– and an extraordinary
thing happened.

The lamplighter did
something no one had ever
seen him do before. He smiled
a sad, faraway sort of smile.

'You'd better come with me,'
he said.

"The lighthouse keeper loved the new fountain,
with its statue of a cat . . ."

# The Family Secret

**O**nce upon a time, there was a lighthouse keeper whose lighthouse had no lamp. The lighthouse had just been built by the Harbour Board of Harbour Heights, a bustling little fishing town which had grown big enough to need one.

Everyone was very proud of the lighthouse at Cyclops Point, which was painted

THE LIGHTHOUSE KEEPER

in fresh red and white stripes and could be seen from all over the little town. Unfortunately, as soon as the sun set, it couldn't be seen from the sea any longer, because it didn't have a lamp. This was because the blacksmith who was supposed to be making it was busy working on another job.

CYCLOPS POINT.

Whenever the lighthouse keeper asked him when the lamp would be ready, the blacksmith would just shrug his shoulders and mutter something about pirates and sea-beds and complicated wrought-ironwork.

Then, one night, there was a terrible storm and the lighthouse keeper felt awful sitting in his lighthouse with no lamp, unable to help the ships out at sea. The very next day he went over to the blacksmith's shop where he found him working on a fountain which he'd just been commissioned to make.

Refusing to accept no for an answer, the lighthouse keeper forced the blacksmith to finish the lamp and to install it at the top of his lighthouse. In return, the lighthouse keeper helped the blacksmith – who was a really skilled craftsman – with the fountain which, when it was completed, was placed in Firefly Field, on the edge of town. The lighthouse keeper loved the new fountain, with its statue of a cat and two seagull spouts, and visited it often – which is where he met a beautiful woman with flashing blue eyes, sitting beneath a tree.

It was love at first sight and, although the woman (who called herself Katherine) was very secretive and wouldn't talk about her past or where she came from, they got married within a week and lived happily ever after in the lighthouse at Cyclops Point.

The years passed and they had a daughter, Molly, who grew up to be as beautiful as her mother – and Harbour Heights grew into a bustling city, visited by lots and lots of ships.

Then one day, when a new automatic lighthouse at Mermaid Cove was opened, the Harbour Board closed the old lighthouse at Cyclops Point. Its lighthouse keeper and his wife put their affairs in order and moved to the Wild West. They were very happy to do this because they had always wanted to retire to a log cabin on the prairie. And besides, their beautiful daughter, Molly, was grown up now and happily married to the story collector, Wilfred McPherson.

MOLLY McPHERSON

It was only after her parents were safely settled in the Wild West that Molly told Wilfred her family secret. Her mother was in fact the notorious pirate captain, Brimstone Kate.

Brimstone Kate had been very ashamed of her past, and had kept it secret, because if anybody had ever found out that she had once been a notorious pirate, then her husband would have lost his job and of course they would have been endlessly bothered by treasure-hunters. But they had put her past behind them, and things had turned out pretty well in the end.

As for Brimstone Kate's treasure, try as they might, the few treasure-hunters who believed that Brimstone Kate hadn't gone down with her ship could never find it. Years later, Brimstone Kate did send a note to her daughter about a one-eyed giant and a one-eared cat – but it got stolen by a slovenly, yet inquisitive, housemaid called Cressida Claw who, try as she might, could make neither head nor tail of it, and in the end gave up trying.

# Chapter Fifteen

obody argued; they just picked up their rugs, suitcases, packing trunks, flotsam and jetsam, and followed the old lamplighter as he *tap-tap-tapped* his way round Firefly Square lighting the lamps, before turning down Brimstone Alley. Nobody argued because nobody knew what else to do.

The lamplighter led them down Brimstone Alley, along Pie Crust Row and through the warehouses and cobbled yards of Harbour Prospect in the lower town. When they reached the harbour itself, he *tap-tap-tapped* his way along the waterfront until they found themselves at Cyclops Point.

There, they climbed the winding steps cut into the rock, up to the old lighthouse. Without a word, the lamplighter approached the lighthouse door, put an old rusty-looking key in the lock and opened it.

'Welcome to my home,' he said in a deep, slightly mournful voice, stepping through the doorway.

Hugo followed the others inside and began to climb the stairs. In front of them, the lamplighter lit the lamps that studded every inch of the circular walls. They were of every shape and size – some, large round globes, others small and delicate. Some had glass covers, others just a naked flame. Edward Evesham whistled through his teeth.

'A man after my own heart,' he whispered.

Reaching the first floor, the lamplighter picked his way through a jumble of driftwood, broken spars, splintered decking, chipped and worn ships' figureheads, and climbed a ladder at the far end. Daisy and Lily Neptune exchanged looks of astonishment as they followed him.

'What a treasure trove!' gasped Daisy.

'Such a discerning collector!' nodded Lily.

At the top of the ladder was the second floor, which resembled the galley of an old pirate ship.

In fact, Hugo noticed, there were two crossed cutlasses above the small window and a tattered-looking flag on one wall with the skull and crossbones on it. In the centre of the room was an old pot-bellied stove with a great brass kettle gently bubbling on it. Freda and Diego Camomile both let out little gasps of delight.

'What a fine-looking stove!' exclaimed Diego. 'And such a magnificent kettle! Perhaps, if you'd permit, we might make everyone a nice cup of tea?'

The lamplighter smiled his sad, faraway sort of smile and nodded.

Hugo left the Camomiles making tea and the Neptune sisters admiring the cutlasses and grappling hooks that hung from the rafters, and followed Meena, Edward and the lamplighter up another ladder to the third floor.

This time it was Meena's turn to gasp. Clasped under her arm, Tik-Tik the moth-dog gave an excited little bark.

They were standing in a room filled with intricately strung hammocks. There were wide hammocks draped with blankets and padded with cushions, smaller hammocks that resembled armchairs, with small slings on which to

rest your feet. There were even hanging tables and bookcases suspended from the ceiling.

'How wonderfully cosy you've made it,' said Meena in her musical voice. 'It's so clever of you!'

'Please,' said the lamplighter, 'make yourself comfortable.'

Meena sat on one of the wide hammocks and Tik-Tik wriggled free, jumped to the floor and ran over to the old lamplighter. He knelt down and tickled the moth-dog behind the ears, his eyes growing misty.

'It's been a long time,' he whispered to Tik-Tik. 'A long, long time. I used to tickle Treacle behind the ear . . .'

'Treacle?' gasped Hugo. 'The one-eared ship's cat?'

The lamplighter smiled and motioned to Hugo and Edward to follow him up the next ladder. This was a lot taller than the others, and led up to a small trapdoor in the ceiling high above.

When Hugo got to the top and clambered through the trapdoor after Edward and the lamplighter, he found himself standing at the very top of the old lighthouse. He gasped with amazement. Through the glass panes of the circular window that ran around the great lamp, Harbour Heights lay spread out before them. Crossing to the other side and pressing his nose against the glass, Hugo stared out at the bright, glistening sea of the harbour.

Far in the distance, a beautiful white liner – the *S.S. Euphonia* – was cutting through the waves, while down by the waterfront, the school ship *Betty-Jeanne* bobbed at anchor. Behind him, Hugo heard Edward Evesham *tut-tutting*. He turned to see the mechanical wizard examining the great lamp with his long, wand-like spanner.

'Seems in perfect working order – except for the turning-mechanism,' he mused to himself. 'Completely jammed . . . Most odd. A lighthouse lamp that can't turn. Now what use is that?'

The lamplighter didn't seem to hear him. Instead he was looking at Hugo with his watery, grey eyes and a mournful expression.

'I was just about your age when I ran away to sea,' he said, crossing to the glass and looking out to sea. 'That was a long, long, long time ago . . .' He shook his grey head and turned to Hugo. 'Would you like to hear my story?'

Hugo nodded.

'Long ago,' the lamplighter began, 'I ran away to sea and became a pirate. You might not think it to

look at me now, but back then – in the old days – I was full of spirit, with a thirst for adventure to match. Well, it wasn't long before I fell in with some bad company and found myself serving as a cabin boy and gunner's mate on the *Lazy*

*Lobster*, a pirate schooner that sailed the seas preying on merchant ships, from the ice straits of the Frozen North to the steamy seas of the Dandoon Delta.

'And what a pirate ship she was! Full of the most fearless desperados that ever set a peg-leg on a plank – and the most fearless and reckless of all was our captain, who went by the name of Brimstone Kate.'

Hugo gulped, and the lamplighter smiled.

'Firm but fair was Brimstone Kate, and she liked me on account of my rescuing the *Lazy Lobster*'s cat from the Dandoon corsairs – even though poor Treacle lost one of her ears. Ships' cats are considered extremely lucky, you see, and pirates are a superstitious lot. Well, after that, Brimstone Kate and the *Lazy Lobster* had a lot of luck, I can tell you. And before long, she was the richest pirate captain of them all. And that, as so often is the case, was when disaster struck, like a black typhoon out of a clear blue sky.'

Frowning with concentration, Hugo listened intently as the lamplighter's voice grew hushed.

'Brimstone Kate put in at Harbour Heights to get a new bed made,' he explained, 'and that took rather a long time. When it was finished we had the difficult task of hauling it back to the ship. It was only after we'd finally got the blasted thing on board and into the captain's cabin that we noticed Treacle was nowhere to be seen. We searched the ship and the streets of Harbour Heights in vain, and were just about to give up when Brimstone Kate herself found Treacle in Firefly Field on the edge of town.

'She'd been caught in a gamekeeper's trap. Poor thing was a ship's cat, not used to the ways of the land. We buried her there and then, and set off that very night. But our luck had run out, and not long after that the *Lazy Lobster* was wrecked on the rocks outside Harbour Heights.

'I managed to swim ashore, but I was the only one. Or so I thought . . . Anyway, by then I'd had enough of the sea, so I became an apprentice to a lamplighter – back in the days when all of Harbour Heights had old lamps that needed lighting. All gone now, of course,' he said, his voice full of regret. 'Replaced by new-fangled lamps . . .'

Edward Evesham flushed red and cleared his throat.

'There's only Firefly Square left now,' the lamplighter added mournfully.

'When did you move into the lighthouse?' asked Hugo, after a brief silence.

'I was just getting to that,' said the lamplighter. 'Years passed and Harbour Heights grew from a little fishing town into a bustling harbour full of ships. One day I was down by the waterfront when I saw an amazing sight. Coming out of the old lighthouse at Cyclops Point, arm in arm with a handsome young man, was a young woman who looked exactly like Brimstone Kate – or rather, exactly as Brimstone Kate had looked when I'd first met her as a young cabin boy. The same flaming red hair, the same dazzling blue eyes . . . You could have knocked me down with a mizzen spar!

'I realized at once that Brimstone Kate hadn't gone down with the *Lazy Lobster* at all.

She must have settled in Harbour Heights, just like me, and that this was her daughter. I found out that the lighthouse was being closed because a new one had been built at Mermaid Cove, and the lighthouse keeper's pretty daughter was getting married to Wilfred McPherson, the story collector.

'Of course, there were rumours that she was the daughter of Brimstone Kate, the notorious pirate captain, and that when she had come ashore, Brimstone Kate had buried her treasure somewhere in Harbour Heights. But no one could actually prove anything, and with both her parents now dead, the poor girl deserved the chance of happiness. So I said nothing. She moved to Firefly Square and had a little daughter of her own.

'I used to see her playing in the gardens around the fountain when I did my rounds. She loved the statue of Treacle. Brimstone Kate had arranged for the same blacksmith who had made her bed to make the statue. Sometime later, it was put over the spot where we found Treacle's body. Occasionally, hopeful treasure-hunters would start digging round it and underneath it, searching for Brimstone Kate's treasure, but they never found a thing, so they all gave up in the end . . .

'So anyway, I moved into Cyclops Point lighthouse when the Harbour Board closed it, and I've lived here ever since.'

The lamplighter turned to Hugo and looked into his face with a quizzical expression in his watery, grey eyes.

'You know,' he said thoughtfully. 'Your eyes – they're the exact same colour as Brimstone Kate's . . .'

# THE FIREFLY QUARTERLY

EDITOR
## ELLIOT de MILLE

ISSUE NUMBER FIFTY-THREE

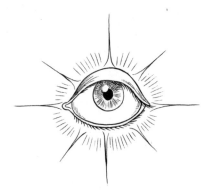

**KEEPING AN EYE ON
HARBOUR HEIGHTS**

# Chapter Sixteen

he shops are all locked and boarded up,' said the lamplighter. He propped his pole against the wall and sat down in a hammock with a heavy sigh. 'And the institute is shut up as usual. I've lit all the lamps – though I don't know why I bothered. Firefly Square is deserted.'

Meena was sitting on a small hammock with Tik-Tik on her lap. Edward Evesham was tinkering with an old lamp in one corner, and the Neptune sisters were examining various interesting pieces of driftwood in another. The Camomiles climbed the ladder, each carrying a tray laden with teacups, a teapot and a large plate of hot buttered toast, and were greeted by murmurs of approval.

Hugo looked around the lighthouse's cosy sitting room. Everybody looked so comfortable and settled, and almost relieved to have left the worries and cares of Firefly Square behind. Even the lamplighter seemed cheerful, and obviously enjoyed the company. The only person not happy and relieved and cheerful was Hugo himself. He let out a long deep sigh. Everybody stopped what they were doing and looked at him.

'Are you all right, Hugo, dear?' said Lily Neptune.

'Not really,' Hugo admitted sadly. 'I mean I'm happy that everything's worked out so well for all of you, but . . .' His lower lip trembled.

'Yes, Hugo, darling?' said Lily. 'What is it?'

'Well,' said Hugo, turning from the small window through which he'd been watching the twinkling lights of Harbour Heights, 'I was just wondering how I'm ever going to get back to Harvi and Sarvi without the snow chariot.

It's up on the roof of *Evesham's Workshop*, which is all locked and boarded up!'

He sat down next to Meena and let out another long, deep sigh. Everybody gathered round, looks of concern on their faces.

'Oh, Hugo, dear!' exclaimed Daisy Neptune. 'We're so sorry. We've been having such a lovely time here in this wonderful lighthouse that we forgot all about you.'

'How thoughtless we are,' said Lily, clucking with concern. 'We must do something to help you.'

'Never fear, Hugo, my lad,' said Edward Evesham. 'If we all pitch in, we can sort this mess out. Now, what you need is a flash lamp, just like this one, so you can see what you're doing . . .'

He placed the lamp on Hugo's head.

'That's a start, at least,' he said, looking round at the others.

Meena got up and slipped from the room.

'And you need courage and a brave heart!' said Freda, passing Hugo a teacup.

'And for that, you must drink my new *Lionheart* tea,' said Diego encouragingly, pouring tea from the teapot.

'A grappling hook!' said Lily, thrusting one into Hugo's arms.

'And rope! Lots and lots of rope!' said Daisy brightly, gathering up a coiled armful.

Everyone gazed at Hugo. Hugo tried to smile back. he knew they meant well, but he couldn't see how any of this was going to help him get into *Evesham's Workshop*.

Then Meena returned, Tik-Tik barking at her heels. 'I've brought you this, Hugo, darling,' she said in her musical voice, holding out a rolled-up carpet. 'It is the only carpet in the world that is made of pure cloud sheep wool. My mother wove it for special occasions when only a hundred per cent pure cloud sheep wool flying carpet would do. This,' she added, 'is one of those occasions.'

Hugo swallowed hard and took the carpet.

'Oh, and Hugo, darling,' said Meena, smiling and slipping off her carpet slippers of unusual design. 'Take these as well, just to be on the safe side.'

Half an hour later, as a full moon rose over Harbour Heights, Hugo stepped off the balcony at the top of the Cyclops Point lighthouse, and onto a gently swaying flying carpet. He sat down gingerly and pointed his toes forward as Meena had instructed him.

'Just point them in the direction you want the carpet to fly,' she called encouragingly. 'And remember, lean forwards for down and backwards for up. It's simple!' she smiled.

'Simple,' said Hugo, trying to stop his knees trembling.

'Your lamp,' said Edward Evesham from the balcony, tapping his own forehead. 'Don't forget your lamp, Hugo, my boy.'

Hugo flicked a switch and the lamp attached to his head flickered into life.

'Good luck!' called Daisy and Lily Neptune.

'Courage, Hugo, lad!' added Diego Camomile.

'Fly safely,' said Meena, letting go of the carpet, which took off instantly on a gust of wind.

Before Hugo knew it, he was sailing high over the harbour towards the broad sweep of Archduke Ferdinand Boulevard. Concentrating with all his might, he pointed his toes towards the left-hand edge of the faded carpet and felt it swoop round in response. He pointed his toes straight ahead and leaned back. Instantly the carpet rose and straightened its course.

Hugo pointed his toes to the left, to the right and straight ahead again, leaning forwards and back, and forwards again. The carpet rose, fell and darted through the air in a lurching zigzag. It was the most exhilarating feeling he'd ever experienced – better even than those first moments in the snow chariot.

It was, Hugo thought dreamily as he soared and swooped through the night sky, almost as if he could fly up and touch the moon.

Just then, a sharp gust of wind made the carpet buckle alarmingly and wobble from side to side. Hugo fell back and clung to the sides as the whole carpet

shot, almost vertically, upwards. For a moment he thought he was going to slide right off it and fall – but he forced himself to lean forwards as far as he could go, and the carpet levelled off once more.

Breathing heavily, and with his heart beating fit to burst, Hugo looked around. Below him lay the grand squares of the Heights, and not far off – in a direct line from the Cyclops Point lighthouse in the distance – lay the twinkling lights of Firefly Square.

Taking a deep breath, Hugo pointed his toes straight ahead and headed for the lights. Leaning forwards, he came down low over Brimstone Alley and flew round Firefly Square in a broad arc. In front of him the shops of the south side drew closer.

He lined up *Evesham's Workshop* with the tips of his toes and, leaning back once more, aimed for the roof.

With a soft swishing sound, the carpet scuffed the roof tiles and came to a skidding halt beside the huge glass skylight, which was propped open. Hugo climbed unsteadily to his feet and pattered across the roof. He looked all round, but there was no sign of the snow chariot, either below in the darkened workshop, or up here on the roof, where it should have been sitting, ready and waiting for him. Hugo glanced down and, as he did so, the light from his head-lamp fell on something that made his heart leap suddenly into his mouth.

There, on the glass of the skylight of *Evesham's Workshop* was a sooty black footprint, as wide as a milk pail and with three long toes splayed out at the front – the footprint of a snow giant!

# THE
# FIREFLY
# QUARTERLY

EDITOR
## ELLIOT de MILLE

ISSUE NUMBER SEVENTY-TWO

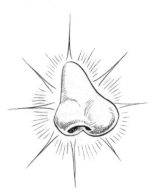

## WITH A NOSE FOR TROUBLE
## IN HARBOUR HEIGHTS

# Chapter Seventeen

or a moment or two, Hugo couldn't believe his eyes. Everywhere he looked, there were more of the sooty footprints. Lots and lots of them. Big and round and three-toed – and, for someone who had grown up in the Frozen North, totally unmistakeable.

'Snow giants?' whispered Hugo, astonished. 'In Harbour Heights?'

He tip-toed across the rooftop. The footprints led to the edge of the roof. Hugo peered across the narrow gap between the roof of *Evesham's Workshop* on the south side, and the roof of the institute on the east side, with the steps of Sleeping Horse Lane between. On the opposite side, the snow-giant footprints continued across the roof of the institute, smeared and smudged here and there by some heavy object being pulled along behind.

'They've made off with the snow chariot,' breathed Hugo.

Taking the grappling hook and rope the Neptune sisters had given him, Hugo threw it across the narrow gap of Sleeping Horse Lane. The grappling hook clattered over the ridge roof of the institute and down the other side of the roof slope. Hugo pulled the rope taut, then clicked his heels. Silently, he rose up and hovered in the air in Meena Dalle's carpet slippers of unusual design. Then, hand over hand, Hugo pulled himself across Sleeping Horse Lane and over the roof of the institute towards a chimney stack. Clicking his heels a second time, he sank gently back down to the roof, landing beside the chimney. He peered over the roof ridge . . .

The snow giant footprints led to a wrought-iron fire escape at the back of the institute. Hugo was just about to follow them when he heard a strange scuffling sound coming up from below. He crouched down behind the chimney stack and, at the very last moment – as the scuffling sound grew louder – remembered to flick his head-lamp off.

The next instant, with a *ploff!* sound, a sooty head appeared out of the chimney pot above Hugo's head.

*Ploff! Ploff! Ploff!*

More heads appeared from the chimney pots all around. Small hairy creatures with long arms, short legs and enormous feet clambered out of the chimneys,  one by one, and padded across the roof tiles. As Hugo watched, they spread out on the roof slope facing Firefly Square and lay down. Then, one by one at first, but soon after in groups of three and four, they raised their enormous feet to the night sky and wiggled their toes at the moon.

Hugo was so astonished he almost slipped and rolled off the roof – but managed to grab hold of the chimney stack and save himself just in time.

'Who'd have thought that snow giants would be so *small*,' he murmured to himself.

For a long while, the creatures lay on their backs, while the cool breeze blowing across the rooftops ruffled the fur of their enormous feet. And as it did so, a low hum – almost like a purr – spread through the crowd.

Hugo remained very still, crouched down behind the chimney stack. It was late now and, what with the humming of the creatures and the gentle, hypnotic sway of their feet, he was beginning to feel a little drowsy. But just as he felt his eyelids growing heavy and his head beginning to nod, something happened that made him sit bolt upright, suddenly wide awake.

The unmistakeable figure of Elliot de Mille, director of the institute, stepped off the fire escape and strode across the roof. He was wearing an expensive-looking silk dressing-gown, slippers of a rather ordinary design – and a look of smug self-satisfaction on his face. When he saw the creatures, he tutted with irritation and clicked his fingers.

'Can't one have even a moment to oneself?' he snapped. 'Bedtime! Lights out in five minutes!'

The contented hum became a low moan as the creatures got to their feet and started shuffling towards the chimney stacks. Elliot de Mille turned his back on them and stared out across Firefly Square. A plump pigeon appeared and landed on the low wall in front of him. Elliot de Mille took the message from its leg and read it.

'Of course, Cressida,' he whispered with a smirk. 'I shall come right away.'

Hugo shrank back behind the chimney stack as the creatures disappeared back down the chimneys.

*Ploff! Ploff! Ploff!*

'I said, five minutes!' barked Elliot, without turning round.

The last creature clambered up onto the chimney stack and disappeared into the chimney pot. Hugo hesitated for a moment, and then – with a last glance at the hunched silk-gowned back of the director of the institute – he clicked the heels of Meena's carpet slippers and rose in the air to the top of the chimney. Carefully positioning himself directly over the chimney pot, Hugo took a deep breath, clicked his heels again and, with a soft sooty *ploff!* of his own, slowly disappeared down inside the chimney.

# THE
# FIREFLY
# QUARTERLY

### EDITOR
## ELLIOT de MILLE

ISSUE NUMBER EIGHTY-EIGHT

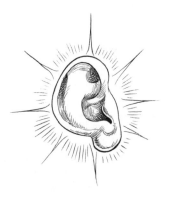

## PUTTING AN EAR TO THE GROUND
## AROUND HARBOUR HEIGHTS

# Chapter Eighteen

ugo gently descended the chimney until his feet touched the fireplace at the bottom. Slowly, he dropped to his knees and peered out into a vast room.

It was full of small beds, the size of babies' cots and arranged in neat lines that stretched into the distance. High above, at the centre of the ceiling, a single enormous light bulb gave off a faint, flickering light. The small hairy creatures were climbing into the tiny beds and pulling the covers over themselves with long thin arms. At the bottom of each bed, two enormous feet stuck out.

Hugo remained crouching in the shadows of the fireplace while the creatures settled. When the last one had climbed into bed, a tiny furry figure with especially enormous feet appeared and made her way along the ranks of tiny beds. Hugo watched as the snow-woman stopped and kissed every one of her two hundred sons goodnight on their furry foreheads, before turning and quietly padding out of the dormitory and turning out the light.

Hugo hesitated. Somewhere in the institute was the snow chariot, and he was determined to find it. He was just about to start creeping through the dormitory when a glow appeared in the distance.

The snowmen all sat up in bed as a figure with a lamp emerged from the shadows at the far end and slowly made its way to the middle of the vast room. There, it produced a cushion, put down the lamp and settled down on the floor. The snowmen crept silently out of their beds and gathered round the figure of an old man with a long flowing beard and a knitted nightshirt. When the little creatures had all sat themselves down, the old man looked round at their expectant, furry faces and cleared his throat.

'Once upon a time . . .' he began, and a contented hum rose through the ranks of listening snowmen.

Hugo settled down to listen, too. The story was about the north wind and his daughter, the ice princess, and a young reindeer herder who fell in love with her and melted her heart. The north wind was angry and blew the reindeer herder far from his home in the Frozen North . . .

Hugo swallowed hard and bit his lip. He had heard this story many times before. It was a story that reindeer herders told their children in front of warm stoves in little cabins deep in the ice forests, as the chill north wind blew outside. It was a story that

Harvi and Sarvi used to tell *him* on long winter nights beneath the ice moon. Hugo's eyes filled with tears.

The young reindeer herder battled through all sorts of dangers and obstacles that the north wind put in his way. As the old man told the story, the snowmen gasped, and hummed; they swayed when the north wind blew and trembled when the icebergs clashed.

Finally the reindeer herder arrived back at his home in the Frozen North – only to find that the ice princess had melted away in her sorrow at losing her beloved. The reindeer herder began to weep and, such was his grief, that he filled a bucket with his tears. The north wind flew into a terrible rage when he discovered that the reindeer herder had returned, and blew himself in a great storm and disappeared over the horizon.

Hugo wiped away a tear of his own and smiled.

When the reindeer herder woke up, the bucket of tears had become an ice forest and the ice princess was waiting for him.

The listening snowmen swayed and shivered and hummed with pleasure as the old man brought his story to a close, picked up the lamp and got to his feet. The snowmen shuffled to their beds, climbed in and pulled the covers back over their furry heads.

'Goodnight, you sons of ice and snow,' whispered the old man as he tip-toed quietly out of the dormitory.

Two hundred soft, snowy snores filled the air as Hugo slipped out of the shadows of the fireplace and tip-toed after him.

# THE
# FIREFLY
# QUARTERLY

EDITOR
## ELLIOT de MILLE

ISSUE NUMBER NINETY-NINE

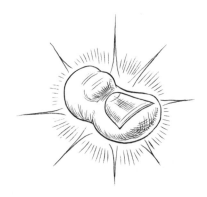

## DIPPING A TOE INTO THE MURKY
## WATERS OF HARBOUR HEIGHTS

# Chapter Nineteen

 ugo followed the old man with the lamp down a long dark corridor, around a corner, down three flights of stairs and into the basement of the institute. The old man opened a door with a glass front and went inside, closing the door quietly behind him. Hugo looked around. The basement was full of large, neat stacks of *The Firefly Quarterly*.

Hugo reached out and took a copy from the nearest pile. He looked at the cover. It was plain and ordinary looking.

It said *THE FIREFLY QUARTERLY* in big letters and ISSUE NUMBER NINETY-NINE in smaller ones. Underneath were the words, EDITOR, ELLIOT de MILLE, above a smaller picture of a big toe. At the bottom of the cover it said, in small sinister letters: DIPPING A TOE INTO THE MURKY WATERS OF HARBOUR HEIGHTS. Hugo shuddered and put the magazine down. No wonder nobody liked *The Firefly Quarterly*, he thought bitterly. It was full of nasty stories, stolen stories; stories that had been twisted out of shape and turned bad. Hugo looked at the neat stacks in the basement of the institute and shook his head sadly. *The Firefly Quarterly* was an ugly, spiteful publication.

He tip-toed to the far end of the dark basement and stopped outside the door. Set into the upper panel was a pane of frosted glass with the words 'Wilfred McPherson, Editor' painted in neat gold letters on it. Hugo hesitated for a moment, then reached out, knocked twice on the door, and opened it.

\*

'Cressida, you've done wonders with the place!' exclaimed Elliot de Mille, walking round the empty shop that had once been *Neptune's Nautical Antiques*.

'Mostly junk of course, but Pingle, Pingle, Duff and Pingle were happy to take it off my hands,' laughed Cressida. 'And pay me a pretty penny for it.'

'I should think so, Cressida,' said Elliot, pulling up an empty tea chest and sitting down beside the old woman. 'After all, I've got plenty of secrets Mr Pingle doesn't want his brothers or Mr Duff to find out!'

They both gave a cackling laugh.

'Cleared the other shops, too,' said Cressida. 'The cats love the carpet shop and the pigeons are roosting in the workshop – and I've got enough tea to last me a lifetime, Alfie, love! Talking of which . . .'

The old woman picked up a teapot with an anchor on its lid and poured tea into the cups on the tea chest between them. 'How about a nice cup of Camomiles' *Tear-Drop* tea?'

Elliot raised his teacup triumphantly. 'Here's to a bright future!' he said, with a thin smile. 'Full of other people's secrets.'

Hugo stepped into the room. It was lined with shelves, hundreds of them, all piled high with copies of *The Firefly Quarterly*. But these weren't like the neat stacks in the basement outside. No, these were

in untidy heaps – some spread out on the floor, others piled high beside them or slotted into the crowded shelves. They had crumpled pages with torn corners and frayed edges, as if they'd been pored over and read many times.

But it was the covers that caught Hugo's eye. They had colourful pictures on them – of flying carpets, blue monkeys, snow giants and exotic birds – and titles that promised of the wonderful stories to be found within. Fables, yarns, myths, tales . . . These magazines were nothing like the ugly ones outside. Hugo could tell just by looking at them that these copies of *The Firefly Quarterly* were beautiful.

'We have a visitor, old friend,' came a voice.

Hugo looked up from the quarterlies at his feet.

There, at a small cluttered desk full of paper and pens and inks and brushes, with a small snowman on his knee, was Wilfred McPherson, the famous story collector.

Hugo smiled. 'My name's Hugo Pepper,' he said. 'And I have a story for you . . .'

\*

'Scrubbing floors, polishing silver, sweeping carpets,' whimpered Cressida Claw, tears streaming down her face and her soggy whiskers quivering. 'No wonder I turned to snooping, Alfie, love. I didn't want to,' she wailed, and took another slurp from her teacup. 'But they drove me to it!'

'That horrible bicycle,' snivelled Elliot de Mille. 'Of course they were going to make fun of me. I mean, wouldn't *you*, Cressida?' He wept bitterly, pouring himself another cupful from the teapot. '... If you saw a butcher's boy on a bicycle with one large wheel and one silly, ridiculous, tiddly, teeny-weeny wheel?' Elliot threw his head back and howled with tears of hurt and self pity. 'I never stood a chance!'

*

'It was the not knowing that was the hardest part,' said Wilfred McPherson, smiling at Hugo and drying his eyes with a large handkerchief. 'Of course, I suspected that something terrible had happened. I could hardly bear it. I lost interest in everything and shut myself up here in my study and lost myself in my beloved stories.'

He shook his head sadly and patted the snowman's furry shoulder.

'Oh, what a stupid, self-pitying old man I have been. I allowed that rascal Elliot de Mille to take over the institute and bully you and your children into printing that awful *Quarterly* of his, didn't I?'

The snowman looked up into the story collector's grief-stricken face and patted his hand.

'Wffl mmfll, wffl wfffl, mmph,' he mumbled softly.

'I know you only did it for me, old friend. It makes me feel terrible, because I was so wrapped up in my own misery that I just didn't care. What did I have to live for with Phyllida and Phineas and their beautiful baby lost for ever?'

Wilfred turned back to Hugo with glistening eyes.

'And now, you, Hugo, my handsome young grandson, have come back to me. It is like waking up from a long, sad, terrible dream. Thank you, Hugo, for telling me your story. You've made a foolish old story collector very happy.'

He got to his feet and took his grandson by the hand.

'Now you must go, Hugo, my boy. Leave at once. The institute is no place for you. Elliot de Mille has poisoned it. It means so much to me that you came back to Harbour Heights, Hugo, but of course I understand that this is not your home. Go back to Harvi and Sarvi in the Frozen North with my blessing.'

RANULF & FINOULA

The storyteller turned to the little snowman and ruffled the hair on his furry head.

'Ranulf, here, will take you to the snow chariot. Finoula and he recognized it as a *Crane and Sons Aeronautical Snow*

*Chariot - Mark II* the moment they saw it on the roof of *Evesham's Workshop*,' he smiled sadly, 'and brought it to me. They thought it might cheer me up. Go now, Hugo, my boy, before Elliot de Mille returns.'

But Hugo shook his head, his bright, clear blue eyes flashing with defiance. Reaching out, he seized a copy of the beautiful *Firefly Quarterly* and held it out to his grandfather.

'This story isn't over,' he said, his voice trembling with emotion. 'And we have all night to give it a happy ending!'

Elliot de Mille dried his eyes with his expensive-looking silk handkerchief and got up.

'I feel much better for that,' he said with a thin smile. 'I can't tell you how good it feels not having to skulk around the square for fear of being recognized any more.'

'It's no more than you deserve, Alfie, love,' said Cressida Claw, her whiskers quivering moistly.

Elliot put on his expensive-looking black overcoat and large silk hat, and was just stepping out of the shop that used to be *Neptune's Nautical Antiques* when he stopped, a look of surprise on his thin, mean-looking face. Across Firefly Square, the windows of the institute were all lit up.

Leaving Cressida Claw looking tearfully after him, Elliot de Mille strode towards the institute, his large silver key in his gloved hand of duck-egg blue. He reached the door and hurriedly put the key in the lock, turned and pushed. But the door wouldn't budge. Elliot de Mille's eyes blazed with anger as he beat on the door of the institute with fists of duck-egg blue.

'What is the meaning of this!' he roared. 'Let me in! *Let me in!*'

The Firefly Quarterly

READ ALL ABOUT IT!

HUGO.

GREAT STORIES ARE BACK!

EDITOR: —100TH ISSUE— ASSISTANT: —
WILFRED McPHERSON    HUGO PEPPER

JOURNAL OF THE INSTITUTE OF TRAVELLERS' TALES.

# Chapter Twenty

lliot de Mille sat on the doorstep of the institute with his head in his hands. He'd spent all night trying to get inside. He had hammered on the door and shouted until his throat was hoarse. He had tried to force open the shuttered windows – and ruined his duck-egg blue gloves. The fire escape had been pulled up and the back doors locked. Now, as the first rays of dawn were breaking over Firefly Square, he was just about ready to give up.

The trouble was, Elliot realized, he'd made the institute just too secure during his time as director, bolting the door and shuttering the windows, and now here he was, locked out himself! All night, the lights inside the institute had blazed, and Elliot had heard a sound that filled him with dread – the *clackety-clack* of the printing presses going at full pelt. Now, as dawn broke, the institute had fallen ominously quiet.

What could it all mean? wondered Elliot de Mille, twisting his silk hat in his hands.

Just then, a curious, stuttering sound started up from the rooftop of the institute above.

*Phut! Phut! Bang! Phut!*

Elliot looked up and his mouth fell open with astonishment. There, sailing up into the dawn sky was an extraordinary contraption – a sort of cross between a sled and a hot-air balloon. Behind it, attached by a rope, the contraption towed a faded-looking carpet. This was all very curious and yet, to Elliot de Mille, it was not the most astonishing thing about the sight.

No, the most astonishing thing to Elliot, was the

sight of Wilfred McPherson, a small boy and a crowd
of snowmen on board, seated next to piles and piles
of what could only be *Firefly Quarterly* magazines.
Elliot gulped like a stranded goldfish as the snowmen
each took a bundle of the journals and threw them
into the air.

The contraption disappeared over the rooftops of Brimstone Alley, heading for the grand squares of Harbour Heights. A moment later, one of the magazines fluttered down and landed at Elliot's feet. He picked it up with trembling hands and looked at the cover.

'GREAT STORIES ARE BACK!' he read, before opening the *Quarterly* and looking at the first page. There, in large letters, was a title that left him trembling from head to toe.

*'THE SAD TALE OF ALFIE SPANGLE, THE BUTCHER'S BOY.'* He read on. *'Once upon a time, there was a butcher's boy called Alfie Spangle . . .'*

Elliot de Mille dropped the *Quarterly*, threw back his head and howled.

*'Noooooo!'*

High above Harbour Heights, the snow chariot sailed, towing the flying carpet behind it. And everywhere it flew – from the grand squares of the Heights, to the alleyways and warehouses of the lower town – copies of the new *Firefly Quarterly* came fluttering down to earth. There, the people of Harbour Heights picked them up as they went about their business.

Soon, there were groups of people from Montmorency Square to Pudding Bowl Row reading and giggling and laughing out loud. But not all were so happy . . .

Bernard Bumble, the meat-pie magnate, wasn't pleased to read about how Elliot de Mille had discovered that his buns were full of sawdust. And at Pingle, Pingle, Duff and Pingle, the bailiffs, a nasty fight broke out.

245

In fact, there were many in the bustling city of Harbour Heights who would have cheerfully wrung the director of the institute's neck if only they could have found him.

But they couldn't, for he, and his accomplice Cressida Claw, had vanished. There was, however, one thing that all the residents of Harbour Heights could happily agree on. The new *Firefly Quarterly* was a great improvement on the old one.

As the moon rose over Firefly Square, the snow chariot came in to land in the gardens, where a small reception committee had gathered. The lamplighter, Daisy and Lily Neptune, Meena Dalle, Edward Evesham and the Camomiles broke into delighted applause as the skis of the chariot touched down on the grass, and Wilfred McPherson and Hugo climbed out. Behind them, small furry snowmen with enormous feet tumbled head over heels as the flying carpet glided down to earth.

'I'm delighted to see you all,' said the old story collector, shaking each of the small group by the hand. 'I'm only sorry I allowed things to go so wrong.'

'Oh, Wilfred!' trilled Daisy and Lily Neptune, embracing him. 'It's just so lovely to see you again. That nasty Elliot de Mille spread the news that you'd retired to the Sunny South!'

'Now we can get back to the way things were,' said Edward Evesham.

'Things can never be quite the way they were,' said Meena sadly, thinking of her best friend. 'But at least now Hugo can return to Harvi and Sarvi in the Frozen North.'

Hugo smiled.

'And we've seen the last of Elliot de Mille,' said Diego Camomile. 'Cleared out of Firefly Square this morning – but not before clearing out all our shops of everything we own. All he left was a dirty teacup.' He pointed to a chipped cup with an anchor design on it which his wife, Freda, was holding.

'*Tear-Drop* tea, by the look of it,' she said, before giving a little ladylike shriek. 'Oh, Diego, I can see it again . . .'

'See what?' said Daisy and Lily Neptune, gathering round as Freda gazed into the bottom of the teacup.

'I see a one-eyed giant,' she said, 'staring at a one-eared cat pointing the way to the sea-bed's treasure.'

'One-eyed giant?' said Daisy.

'One-eared cat?' said Lily.

'Sea-bed's treasure!' said Hugo, excitedly. 'I think *I* might know what that means!'

A little while later, a flying carpet ridden by a young woman with a moth-dog on her lap dropped an old lamplighter and a mechanical wizard off at the top of the old lighthouse at Cyclops Point and flew off. Back in the gardens of Firefly Square, an extraordinary collection of people waited by the old fountain with the statue of a one-eared cat holding a curled scroll in its paws.

There was the stooped old story collector with the careworn face and sad eyes. There were the little furry snowmen, the toes of their enormous feet tapping with barely concealed anticipation, and the tall elegant mermaids, whose tails tapped also, beneath the silken folds of their long walksuits. Beside them, the tea blenders from the Sunny South stood arm in arm, their eyes fixed on the Cyclops Point lighthouse in the distance. The small boy dressed in the costume of a reindeer herder from the Frozen North, and clutching a large shovel, turned and gave them all a dazzling smile.

The next moment, the great lamp at the top of the lighthouse burst into life for the first time in many, many years. All over Harbour Heights, people leaned over balconies, or peered from open windows, or looked up from their copies of *The Firefly Quarterly* as they sat in cafés or on park benches.

High over the rooftops of Montmorency Square and Clifftop Row, of Archduke Ferdinand Boulevard and Harbour Side, of Sleeping Horse Lane and Brimstone Alley, the one-eyed giant sent its dazzling beam of light.

Down it shone, cutting through the darkening sky from the distant lighthouse, directly into the small overgrown gardens at the centre of Firefly Square. There, the beam of light struck the curled bronze scroll held in the claws of the one-eared cat that perched on top of the old disused fountain.

Bouncing off it, the light shot across the gardens like a glowing finger, pointing the way. It fell on a patchy piece of grass directly beneath a tall, spreading tree in the corner of the gardens: the very tree that Hugo Pepper had landed in just a few short days before.

Hugo rushed to the spot and began to dig. A few moments later, the edge of his shovel hit something hard and metallic – something like a very, very large treasure chest . . .

*CLINK!*

# Epilogue

From the *Montmorency Gazette:*

# Montmorency Gazette

## FIREFLY FELINE SHINES ON PIRATICAL PLUNDER

*(By our own correspondent)*

Amid amazing scenes last night, the mythical treasure of the notorious pirate, Brimstone Kate, was finally unearthed by an enterprising visitor from the Frozen North. Hugo Pepper, 12, said yesterday, 'Treasure-hunting is just my cup of tea!'

For years, treasure-hunters have searched Harbour Heights, digging up Arthur Bluntstone's blacksmith shop, and looking beneath the cat fountain in Firefly Square. But it was only when Hugo Pepper had the bright idea of firing up the old Cyclops Point lighthouse that a fresh light was shone on the problem. The statue of Brimstone Kate's cat reflected the beam of light directly on the spot where the pirate had hidden her plunder.

The grateful Harbour Board have rewarded the young reindeer herder with half the two thousand and twenty-two gold Dandoon doubloons, which the young treasure-hunter intends to use to commemorate his parents, who were tragically eaten by polar bears.

From the *Harbour High Society* magazine:

## Seagull ABOUT TOWN

### STATUE HONOURS THE MEMORY OF 'THE PEPPERS OF FIREFLY SQUARE'

A new statue was unveiled in Firefly Square of the brave young story collectors, Phineas and Phyllida Pepper, by their son, Hugo, 11 years after they were tragically eaten by polar bears in the Frozen North. Their story has since become famous as the basis for the musical drama 'The Peppers of Firefly Square'.

From a theatre poster outside the
Archduke Ferdinand Theatre:

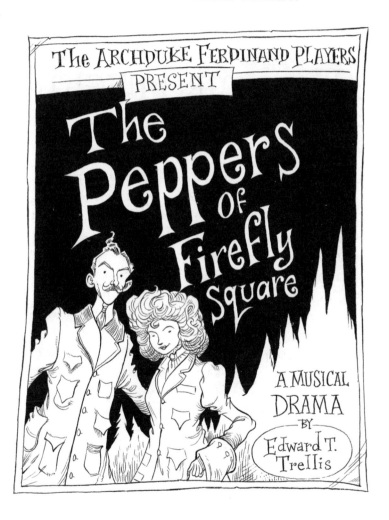

From *The Harbour Heights Grocer*:

# The HARBOUR HEIGHTS ~ GROCER ~

After the shock news of the collapse of Bernard Bumble's meat pie empire, the Grocer is happy to report some good news. World-renowned cheesemakers of the Frozen North, Harvi and Sarvi Runter-Tun-Tun are opening a cheese shop in our fair city. Runter-Tun-Tuns' Reindeer Cheese of Firefly Square – turn right out of Sleeping Horse Lane, first shop on the east side.

The Runter-Tun-Tuns intend to spend the winters in Harbour Heights selling the cheese they make all summer in their little cabin in the ice forests of the Frozen North.

The shopkeepers of Firefly Square told the Grocer, 'We're delighted to welcome the Runter-Tun-Tuns to our little family.'

From the school magazine of the
school ship *Betty-Jeanne*:

## THE SCOWLING MERMAID

### SUMMER TERM

We are pleased to welcome Hugo Pepper,
grandson of Wilfred McPherson of the
Institute of Travellers' Tales, to our
school this term. Hugo has recently
returned from the Frozen North with
Harvi and Sarvi Runter-Tun-Tun,
the famous cheesemakers. Headgirl,
Corby Flood, said, 'Hugo has quite
a story to tell!'

# Hugo Pepper's Family Tree:

Message received by flying box by Edward
Evesham of *Evesham's Workshop*:

Dear Edward,
I need your help,
am coming to see you
in Firefly square,
your old friend,
Theo
Crane.

PAUL STEWART is a highly regarded author of books for young readers – everything from picture books to football stories, fantasy and horror. Several of his books are published by Random House Children's Books, including *The Wakening*, which was selected as a Pick of the Year by the Federation of Children's Book Groups. Together with Chris Riddell, he is co-creator of the bestselling *Edge Chronicles* series, which is now available in over thirty languages. *Fergus Crane*, the first in their Far-Flung Adventures sequence, won a Smarties Prize Gold Medal and *Corby Flood* won a Nestlé Prize Silver Medal.

CHRIS RIDDELL is an accomplished graphic artist who has illustrated many acclaimed books for children, including *Pirate Diary* by Richard Platt, for which he won the 2001 Kate Greenaway Medal, *Something Else* by Kathryn Cave, which was shortlisted for the Kate Greenaway Medal and the Smarties Prize and won the Unesco Award, and *Castle Diary* by Richard Platt which was Highly Commended both for the 1999 Kate Greenaway Medal and for the V&A Illustrations Award. Together with Paul Stewart, he is co-creator of the bestselling *Edge Chronicles* series, which is now available in over thirty languages. *Fergus Crane*, the first in their Far-Flung Adventures sequence, won a Smarties Prize Gold Medal and *Corby Flood* won a Nestlé Prize Silver Medal.

WILFRED MCPHERSON

WILFRED MCPHERSON, renowned academic explorer and story collector, has travelled to the farthest of far-flung places in his pursuit of myths, fables and extraordinary tales. Published in *The Firefly Quarterly*, the esteemed journal of travellers' tales, they are loved the world over. Wilfred McPherson is also the patron of the P.S.P.P.S. (Pygmy Snowmen Printers Preservation Society).